BENDER AT THE BON PARISIEN

BENDER
AT THE
BON
PARISIEN

Pres Maxson

Edited by Jennifer Maxson and Lauren Lastowka

For Mollie, Cece, and Josie

Chapter I.

I was overthinking the architecture. One of the ceiling corners of our small, antique-white hotel room included no right angles. Either the floor above us was tilting, or the walls were folding toward each other. I blinked, trying to force my eyes to focus on it. It was early, and Janie was still asleep.

We'd left the window open overnight. A car door slammed six stories below on the Rue de l'Échelle. The first hues of light created subtle shadows in our room.

Janie lay still and small beside me. We had been married for two years, and I still thought she was classically cute. She had a playful spirit and somehow looked mischievous even when she slept.

I imagined the city outside. Soon the morning fog would loosen its grip around the steel skeleton of the Eiffel Tower. Its exit from the city would resemble a slow march, ghosts leaving the grand avenues crisp and clear. I guessed ponds in the parks were impossibly still. Shop fronts remained dark save the occasional boulangerie, baking the morning's bread under soft yellow lights.

As I gingerly swung my feet off the bed, something pulled me toward the window. My body lifted itself. The carpet was thin and cool, the air slightly biting. Delicately dizzy, I still felt the few bottles of wine we split at dinner the evening before.

The window was large enough to be a doorway. Beyond our small wrought iron railing, the Paris morning was still a sunless, glowing phosphorescent grey. I could make out images below, but without my glasses, the street in the low light looked like a charcoal drawing, vague and dark.

Rooftops across the way were about even with our window. Beyond them, more roofs crested as if they were approaching in waves. Black windows with flower boxes lined up like the same photograph over and over on a page in an album. Traffic lights below flashed for no one.

I scanned the sidewalk directly opposite our hotel. My eyes had begun to regain their focus power. I could identify the figure of a man standing under an archway over an alley, off the sidewalk below. Still sleepy, I thought I might be imagining him.

I didn't think too much of the stranger at first. The city still slept, and all seemed normal. There wasn't another person in view, no café owner sweeping their storefront entrance, no moving vehicles.

Yet there he stood, his eyes apparently fixed on a spot somewhere beneath me, on our side of the street. Was something happening in front of our hotel? If it were, I couldn't hear it, and he wasn't reacting. He stood expressionless, silent, and still.

The man didn't shift his stance once. His suit was smart and casual, but distance and darkness obscured details about his face or age. Was he waiting for someone? No coffee. No cigarette. No paper.

Was I sure that I wasn't dreaming him? He seemed out of place. Finally, as if sensing my unease, his head turned slowly upwards. Our eyes met.

"Hey Pete," Janie whispered sweetly from the bed behind me.

She broke my trance. I turned to look at her. She was propped up on one elbow, wearing one of my undershirts, and gently brushing her straight brown hair out of her face.

"Hey baby," I answered.

"What are you doing?"

Her voice sounded beautiful even when groggy.

"I was just looking down at the street," I stammered, as I turned back to the window. The man was gone. I tilted my head like a dog staring at an inchworm. I swear I'd barely taken my eyes away for a second. "Huh," I grunted.

"What is it?" Janie asked.

"Nothing. Just saw a guy down there."

"A guy?"

"Thought I did at least."

"Was he bringing us coffee?" she laughed, slumping back to her pillow.

"Hopefully?" I answered, smirking.

"Can we sleep in a little longer?" Janie asked as she rolled over. Her hair spread out on the pillow, floating as if underwater.

"Of course."

"Are you coming back to bed?"

"Yep," I said still without moving, focusing again on the archway below. Maybe the man hadn't been there at all. Perhaps he was just a distant image from some lost memory, superimposed on the scene by my exhausted mind.

Still, there was that brief, arresting moment of eye contact. It felt as if no distance had existed between us. The effect would have been the same had we been standing opposite each other in a doorway, unsure which one of us should step aside to allow the other to pass.

I tried to forget about him. I went back to the bed but didn't fall asleep. Janie woke up for good soon after. She put on a short denim skirt over black leggings. I accidentally skipped a buttonhole on the first try with my favorite blue plaid shirt.

My head cleared and mind focused, making me once again question the ghost standing beneath the archway on the sidewalk earlier. I also reexamined the corner of our small, antique-white hotel room. This time, the floor and ceiling appeared to be perfectly parallel.

*   *   *

Having met in college, Janie and I hit it off as a bartender-waitress pair in a college-town bar. She was now a grad student in poetry and often wore colors that clashed. I busied myself trying to be professional as a junior staff writer for the Indianapolis Star. We'd saved for more than a year for France.

Janie's hair, tied back and looking like tail feathers, bounced in front of me as we walked down the winding stone staircase to the lobby. The Hôtel des Bretons was reminiscent of a rundown museum. Original rich reds in the artwork and interior design had faded to maroons. Distant doors echoed as they open and shut, augmenting the silence. We hadn't seen any other guests though, nor did we care if there were any.

Paul, the pleasant salt-and-pepper-haired concierge normally greeted us with a smile and a nod, but he wasn't at his post. It must have been too early. A young clerk with dark eye makeup read her book behind the front desk and didn't look up as we walked passed. Our steps echoed in the high-ceilinged entryway.

Motion caught my eye. A red curtain swayed across a doorway off the lobby. I'd only caught a fleeting glimpse of him, but I was almost sure that I'd just seen the man from the sidewalk dart through it. There wasn't enough time for a double take. Janie heard me gasp.

"What is it?"

"I don't know," I said as we walked. A 'closed' sign stood in front of the curtain. I hadn't noticed this doorway before in our comings and goings. "I swear I just saw that guy from the street this morning."

"Who?"

"The one I told you about."

"Wow, I barely remember that," she answered.

I had to look in.

"Are you sure you just saw someone?" she continued. "I mean, I didn't hear anything or see anybody."

"I don't know," I mumbled.

Without the concierge there to stop me, I crept passed the sign and peered between the doorjamb and curtain. Quiet and magnificent, what lay inside was instantly intriguing.

"What is it?" Janie asked.

"It's a bar."

"Huh, I didn't know this hotel had a bar."

"Me neither," I muttered.

"Been here two days, you'd think somehow we'd have seen that," Janie remarked, pushing herself under my arm. My chin rested on the top of her head.

We could see the entire inside of the room from the doorway. Hanging glassware shimmered. Dark worn woods made the room smell like the inside of a drawer. Lines of liquor bottles stood in perfect rows, light passing through each magnificently. Knickknacks peppered the shelving among the bottles, almost giving the wall the look of an antique store. An eclectic and crooked mix of decorative hangings and artwork covered every inch of wall space. The bar fit just five or six stools, but many tables filled out the rest of the room all the way to the front windows, facing the street corner. An exterior exit across the room was presumably locked. The stranger from the archway was nowhere to be found.

"He really is a ghost," I mused under my breath. Janie didn't hear me.

"This place is perfect," she said.

"It's immaculate," I echoed.

"I don't see anyone."

"Me neither."

Janie thought for a moment. "Let's try this out tonight when it's open."

"Sounds good." Turning back to the clerk in the lobby, I asked, "Excuse me. Have you seen anyone else down here this morning?"

"No. You are the first guests up," Dark Eyes responded, looking up from her book for the first time.

I was puzzled.

"Strange," Janie said, turning away from the curtain. "Ready?"

"Yeah. I need a coffee. I think I'm seeing things."

We left the Hôtel des Bretons and disappeared into the soft morning light, bound for a café.

*   *   *

That afternoon, I'd intended to relax and read at the hotel. I must not have lasted more than a few paragraphs, because I woke up just before dinnertime with the book resting on my chest. It was open to the same page on which I'd started.

"I don't need to take the elevator this time," Janie said, as we walked the narrow hallway to the stairs. It was the size of a phone booth and sounded like grinding teeth. I rubbed my eyes and yawned.

"You need to wake up. Lots of night left."

"I'll be fine," I grunted, looking forward to food and drink.

Each step on the staircase felt well trodden, the stone gently worn down from decades of soles. When we arrived in the lobby, the concierge sat on a tall chair at his post.

"Good evening," he greeted us pleasantly with a nod.

"Paul! Good evening!" I answered before the curtained doorway caught my eye again. The 'closed' sign was still up.

"Will this be open tonight?" I asked him, already feeling energized.

"The Bon Parisien? No, I'm sorry sir. We do not have a bartender right now."

"Ah," I nodded.

"That might explain why we haven't noticed it. It hasn't been open," Janie wondered aloud.

"I could have sworn I saw someone go in there this morning," I continued to Paul.

"Perhaps," he answered. "The exterior entrance has been locked for a few weeks, but it could have been a hotel staff member."

"Maybe," I answered, doubting it.

Janie and I continued with a step toward the exit, but something stopped me. Visions of happy hour in our own private Parisian bar flourished.

"Well, may I have the job tonight?!" I blurted out.

The concierge laughed. "Very good, monsieur."

"No I'm serious," I gently persisted. "Maybe one drink before dinner?"

Obviously it was an unlikely request from a guest, but I could tell he was thinking.

"I have experience as a bartender, so I wouldn't make a mess. I did it in college," I added.

He tried not to smile at my poor pronunciation.

"Of course, we'll pay for it," I insisted.

Paul began to lift his hand to wave us out to the sidewalk. He started to shake his head.

"I'll make you one too," I tried with a smile.

Surely with denial on the tip of his tongue, he then glanced toward the front desk clerk. It wasn't Dark Eyes. This man stood smiling under his bowl haircut.

I couldn't tell if they were humoring or silently laughing at me. The clerk didn't say anything, but he nodded slightly.

"Go ahead," Paul said with sigh. "We've had a gate up all week until a day or so ago, and it'll be nice to see someone using the bar again."

"Great! I'll get you a beer!" I blurted out, suddenly ecstatic.

"I don't need a drink, but I'll be right in behind you shortly," he kindly answered.

I turned to Janie, unable to mask my giddiness.

"What just happened?" She asked. "Are they open tonight?"

"No, but I asked if we could go in."

"He said yes, didn't he?"

"Yep."

"Awesome," she said with a smile.

We walked around the 'closed' sign, and our evening in the Bon Parisien was underway. Excitement made me temporarily forget any person or ghost I may have imagined earlier. However, we'd soon learn that many corners of Paris are home to complicated, even enchanted, histories.

I pulled aside the curtain and stepped in.

Chapter II.

"The light switch is just on your right," the concierge called from behind.

I reached into the darkness. "I found it, thanks."

As I turned up the dimmer, the bar immediately felt warmer. Janie ventured by me. She slid on to a barstool and rested her feet on the crossbar, worn through the stain to raw wood.

I've always been in love with bars. They are hives for conversation, albeit often drunk and meandering ones. Low-hanging lights, the buzz of cheap neon signs, and dusty bookshelves attract me. I'm not a regular anywhere specific at home, but the Bon Parisien checked every box on my list.

"Well? Make me a drink!" Janie urged. She was having fun.

I moved behind the bar and started to take inventory. Just like the wallpaper in the hallways upstairs, many of the labels on the bottles were peeling at the corners.

"What may I make you?" I asked, putting my hands on the bar. The dark wood was covered in so many coats of varnish that I almost suspected it wasn't ever an actual tree.

"Surprise me. We're on vacation."

I found some gin. I set the bottle on the counter and flipped a nearby highball into position next to it.

"Fancy," she noted.

I smiled as I worked.

"Be careful, please," came Paul's voice from the doorway.

"Sorry. Old habit."

"It looks like you are comfortable here. Please find me if you need anything."

"Are you sure that I can't make you something?" I asked one last time.

"Thank you very much. I'm working," he kindly replied. Part of me thought that he wouldn't have accepted even if he were off the clock.

"Of course," I answered.

"I'll come back in shortly. Enjoy yourselves." With that, the concierge exited the bar and shifted the curtain closed behind him.

"Is this 'the dream' or what?" I said.

Janie laughed.

"Remember reading a book as a child about some kids getting locked in a department store?" I asked.

"Rings a bell," Janie nodded.

"I think this is the equivalent." I looked around. "Ice."

Beneath the bar, a dry and empty metal bin sat holding a metal ice scoop, but I saw something else that distracted me. Hung ceremoniously in the dim underworld of the bartender's workspace, a rifle rested upon a pair of tarnished brass hooks. Janie noticed the surprise in my eyes.

"What?"

"There's a gun under here." I had never seen a gun in any of the bars where I had worked before. I instinctively leaned in for a closer look.

"What kind of gun?" Janie asked curiously.

"A rifle."

"Well let's see it."

"Oh God, no, honey. I'm not touching it!" I exclaimed.

"I could take your picture while you're holding it if you want," she said.

"Are you kidding, why would I do that?"

"I don't know. You're a dude, and dudes like guns."

"This thing scares the crap out of me. What if it had been used to kill someone? I don't want my fingerprints all over that thing!"

"Fine, have it your way," she conceded.

"Do you want your picture with it?"

"No! I'm not touching it," she said with a giggle.

I laughed. "Okay then." I turned to search for ice again.

"I guess that's life as a bartender in the big city," she said.

"Yeah, I guess. I hope no one's ever had to use it," I answered.

"At least tell me what it looks like while you're making me a drink."

I glanced down one more time. "Well, it is pretty serious given our location. It's a shotgun. That would do an insane amount of damage in here. Why not conceal a handgun back here?"

"Maybe the bartender was a terrible shot?" Janie joked, referring to the lack of accuracy needed to hit a target with buckshot.

I spied a small refrigerator in a dark corner and went to it. "I'm just going to pretend that gun isn't there," I said.

"Good plan."

The interior of the fridge was packed with chilled beers. In the freezer area, I found one ice cube tray that was only about half full. "Whoa. We'll have to be frugal with the ice."

"Oh, that's okay. We'll just have one here before we head out for dinner," Janie answered.

I dropped three cubes into her glass, took another two for myself, then refilled the tray and put it back for the next tourist bartender.

"Gin and tonic?" I asked Janie.

"Are you serious?"

"What?"

"That night with the accordion? I'll never drink a gin and tonic again."

I laughed. Months earlier, we'd been out with friends. Janie drank many gin and tonics, and the night ended in our apartment as she sang loudly in the bathtub. I sat on the toilet seat, playing along on a toy accordion.

"Besides," she continued, "we are in the heart of Paris, locked in our own little bar, fully stocked with tons of booze we've never heard of, and you want to make a simple little gin and tonic?"

"Okay," I answered. "What do you suggest?"

"I don't know. You're the pro. If you ask me, we should invent something."

"Really?"

"Totally. Then, we can always drink it and remember tonight."

"Okay," I thought aloud as I looked over the liquor. "I love whiskey."

"I know. I like it alright, but there's got to be more to it than that."

"Here's something with a picture of an apple on it. I don't recognize the wording in French on the label though."

"I like apple things," Janie said.

I unscrewed the top of the bottle and sniffed. It was apple alright, and it stung. I poured a small amount over the whiskey in the glasses I'd prepared.

"Add bitters," Janie suggested.

"Really? Why?"

"I don't know. I've just heard of bartenders using them before."

"Do you even know what bitters are?" I asked.

"No. Do you?"

I laughed. "I actually don't. They add pretty rich flavor, but I don't know the spices or flavors involved. So you got me. But we have some back here."

The drink's light amber hue was stained with dark wispy clouds as I added a few drops of bitters. Janie took her drink from me and swirled the ice in the glass. She sniffed it and nodded approval.

"Well, here we go, baby," she said.

"Cheers, honey."

After a small taste, she nodded again. "It's really not bad. Nice job."

"Yeah, I like it. What should we call it?"

"I'll leave it up to you. You are the one who mixed it."

"How about an Esprit de la Nuit."

"Spirit of the night? I like it." She took another drink. "Is it really already quarter to eight?"

"What? No," I answered, looking at my watch. "It's not even six thirty yet."

"Okay, that's what I thought. Just got confused by the clock behind you."

"I noticed that. It's nice. Too bad it's broken," I answered as I turned to the timepiece. The clock, suspended at 7:45, was ornate and looked slightly newer than most of the décor. The design on the face was unique, with silver and gold carvings of the sun and moon. I'd never seen one like it and imagined that it should go on a rich person's mantle.

"All the trinkets behind you," Janie said, forgetting about the clock, "looks like a pawn shop back there."

"You're right. Nothing matches. The plaques, the pictures."

I looked around a little more. An old black-and-white checkered flannel shirt was tucked away beneath the bar. It was out of character with the style of the place. But I kept an extra shirt stashed behind the bar when I was a bartender, so I can't say that I was surprised. An old pair of lace-up construction boots also sat beneath the bar. These made less sense to me, but everything in the room was a little eclectic.

"What about that record player?" Janie asked as she glanced toward the end of the bar over my far shoulder.

I shifted my gaze. Cobwebs marred the view through the dingy clear lid. I imagined for just one moment that it didn't even need a record to play, that if the needle dropped on nothing, sounds of the bar's past would suddenly come alive.

"I wonder if it plays," I said almost to myself.

"Do you think this place had regulars?"

"Sure, don't you think?"

"Probably a bunch of old folks," she guessed with a shrug. "I think I'm probably going to write a lot about this place when we get back."

"Seems perfect for that."

"Did you see the piano over there?"

I looked up. Sure enough, a dusty upright grand lurked in the shadows.

"Yeah, cool," was all I mustered.

"You should play it."

"I might give it a whirl." I wasn't very good.

"I know you want to," she coaxed before looking back at the shelves behind the bar. "Who do you think that is?"

Glancing over my shoulder, I noticed a bronze bust holding court over the room. The character frowned, adding ice to his glassy stare. It was about the size of my fist and looked like a bookend without a matching second half.

"I don't know, but he seems to think he's someone," I joked, noting his expression.

"Maybe a king?"

"I'm not sure. Wouldn't royalty have some sort of crown?"

"Who knows? Weren't they all weird people?"

"I think I'm going to get an artist to make a bust of me."

Janie smiled. "Why?"

"Don't you think that it would be cool? Maybe I'll give it to you for your birthday."

She laughed. "Great. Just what I always wanted."

"I think I'd do the same look on my face as this guy," I said, motioning to the small statue.

"He's more sophisticated than you," she shrugged.

"A guy like that does what he wants."

"He does look proud of himself," she added. "Hey, may I come back there?"

"Of course. I don't work here," I joked.

"I've never been behind an actual bar before."

"How is that possible?"

"I'm not actually sure." Her interest was evident as she made her way around slowly, relishing the moment.

"So what do you think?"

"It's excellent," she said as she looked around and placed both hands on the counter as if she were surveying an imaginary party.

"Do you feel powerful?"

She laughed and turned to me. I went in for a kiss. She patted my back the way she does during a kiss that isn't supposed to last long.

"Pretty cool night, Mister Pete," was all she mustered before pulling away from me.

"Sure is," I whispered.

"I got you something!" she exploded suddenly.

"What?" I said with surprise. "No you haven't."

"No, I did," she said smiling.

"What is it?"

"Just a little token to remember tonight."

"I have a feeling I'll always remember tonight anyway."

"Do you want it now, or later?"

"Yes, now please. What is it?"

"I shouldn't have said anything. It would be so much better if I'd waited to give it to you later."

"Well it's too late now," I laughed. "What is it?"

"It's this little guy!" Janie exclaimed as she pulled a figure out from behind her back. Carved from stone, I recognized it as a rendering of Rodin's sculpture of Balzac. Only a few inches high, he stood naked and defiant.

"Balzac?" I asked.

"Yep. A little Balzac."

"Where did you get him? I don't remember seeing him at a souvenir shop."

"I took him from the shelf right here," she answered, pointing between the bottles.

"Oh, c'mon. Don't steal him."

"No one will miss him. It'll be fine."

"Are you sure this is a good idea?"

"C'mon, Pete. I'm sure someone left him in here by accident in the first place."

"I don't know," I said, looking him over.

"I'll leave a few extra euros for him along with the drink money. Does that make you feel better?"

"Okay, you got me," I answered, thrusting Balzac into the pocket of my corduroys.

"That reminds me," Janie looked around. "Is there an envelope or anything back here? We should keep track of how much we spend. You know, put money in as we go."

"Well, how much longer are we going to stay? I figured we'd head out to dinner shortly."

"Yeah I know. But, I could handle one more so I think we should keep track. You know, not betray Paul's trust."

"Right," I agreed.

Finding an envelope with the words "theatre tickets" scribbled on it stashed behind the register, I scratched out the existing label and replaced it with our room number. We stuffed a few euros inside.

"There. I feel better about taking Balzac now," I said.

"He'll look good on our bookshelves at home."

Suddenly, the front door to the street rattled. Someone was trying to open it from the outside. We saw the shadow of a large dark figure peering into our date. It knocked on the window twice, but I waved them off.

"Sorry! Closed!" I shouted. It had been an aggressive sort of shake. After the door rattled again, the shadow moved away. "I guess the lights attract customers," I mused.

"I guess so," Janie answered. "So what's for dinner?"

"Oh, I don't know. We could try any number of the little places right out along here."

"Let's ask Paul. I didn't love lunch yesterday," Janie admitted.

"What was wrong with lunch yesterday?"

"It was gross."

"I loved it!" I said. Having never used a two-pronged fork before, I'd had orange duck and a pilsner.

"Well, we shouldn't just randomly choose somewhere, is my point. We have no idea that way if a place is actually good."

"It's Paris. It's all good," I ventured.

"Please. I mean, if we're on vacation, it's worth taking a little extra effort to find something really special."

"Okay, that makes sense."

"You want it to be good, right?"

"Of course."

The curtain ripped open, and a very large woman strode into the bar. The concierge was right behind her, unable to stop her.

"The front door is locked!" She sang in French as she passed a few tables and pulled a chair away from the bar. "This alone is offense enough for me to …"

"I'm sorry Madame von Hugelstein. We are closed this evening," Paul began.

"Then what is this?" she yelled indignantly. "Do you select your patrons now that you are in charge? Victor would not have allowed this!"

Janie and I glanced at each other. The woman looked ridiculous with her fur coat and plumed purple hat. Her eyes pointed in different directions.

"I'm sorry, madame, these are our guests. They are simply having a look around before dinner," Paul explained.

"They are having a drink!" she exclaimed as she looked at me. "They are not looking around! They are having a fête!"

"It's not a big fête," I interjected. "We're just enjoying this lovely room for a minute. We're actually about to leave."

"AMERICANS?!" she exploded after detecting multiple imperfections in my French. "Paul, you foul animal. You are staining Victor's memory!"

Paul rolled his eyes.

Again, I attempted to help. "May I make you a drink before dinner, madame?"

She shot me a disparaging look. I glanced over at Paul, and he looked back, defeated. He lazily thrust his hand in the air as if he barely had the strength to lift it.

"One," he said.

"Whiskey," she hissed. "No Scottish swill."

I looked for a bottle with a label all in French. "Is this one okay?" I asked.

"Two ice cubes, and a little vermouth."

I knew that she meant a Manhattan. I was not going to point out the name of the drink. "I'm sorry, madame, we don't have any more ice right now."

"Well that's perfect. Of course you don't."

"Will you take it neat?" I asked.

"I think I'll have to."

Our guest was a cartoon of herself. We were doing our best to hide our amusement, but I noticed Janie snicker. I slid the concoction toward the woman, who took an expressionless slip.

We sat in silence for a few seconds. Janie and I exchanged a few silent words. I thought that we could inhale the Esprits de la Nuit and move on. The evening's enjoyment beckoned and we could feel ourselves wading into bizarre waters if we stayed longer.

Madame von Hugelstein didn't say a word. She stared off in another direction, perhaps viewing a corner of her mind that was alien to us. Or, she was doing the same thing we were: avoiding eye contact. I decided to accelerate the exchange.

"Well, we were about to go get some dinner ..."

"Victor was a good man," she spat.

I sighed, seeing that she didn't care about our dinner.

"I'm sorry, who is Victor?" I asked. At the moment, I didn't know whether I actually cared or just wanted to finish the conversation quickly.

"The bartender here, of course. You're standing on hallowed ground!"

"Where is he?" I asked. "We heard this place has been closed for a while. Did he quit?"

"No, no," she sighed. "He has probably run off with some tramp."

"Oh, uh, okay. Were you two close?"

"Absolutely, but it's been a few weeks," she said, still avoiding direct eye contact.

Janie and I shared a look again.

"Are you from the neighborhood?" I asked.

"Yes. I live a few streets down. I am an opera singer."

That explained the downright melodic sounds of her outburst as she entered the room minutes earlier.

"Oh wow, that's great," I said trying to lighten the situation.

"Pete plays a little piano," Janie added.

"Well, not really. I am a writer. Well, a journalist, really."

The woman didn't react.

"Give yourself some credit, baby," Janie replied. "He's better than he says he is. He was in a rock band once."

"Well, we only played one gig. It was freshman year of college," I answered. "Still, it was a good place. For Indiana."

"I don't know where that is," the opera singer mumbled into her drink.

"It's in the middle of the U.S.," I answered. "I'm sorry, I'm not sure that I caught your name. It was Madame von …?"

"Hugelstein. Trudel von Hugelstein," she said with a nod but without a smile or kind tone. She bit into the second half of her last name and emphasized the shteen.

"von Hugelstein? Is that German?"

"I'm French, asshole!" she struck.

"I apologize." There was a little more silence.

"Victor knew that I was French the day that I met him."

"I'm sorry. I don't know what I was thinking," I said, back-peddling.

She took a sip of her drink.

"We were in love. Or, at least I thought we were in love."

Here we go, I thought. Janie shot me a look.

"She was in love with the bartender here before he took off," I whispered in English.

"No, I think I got it. Bummer," Janie commented, slowly stirring her Esprit de la Nuit with a short straw.

Trudel picked up her drink and stood. "It's amazing how terrible this place has become in just a few weeks. Look at all this dust."

I hadn't noticed it. Everything looked clean to me.

"What kind of bartender are you?" she added as she looked around. "Get a rag. Fix this." She motioned grandly toward the room.

Janie looked like she enjoyed hearing this stranger boss me around. She raised her eyebrows and smiled. I wet a bar towel and came out from behind the counter, not willing to clean up the entire place. I wiped down one table and righted the chair. The clock chimed behind me. I turned to see Trudel, who was now engaged behind the bar.

"This room isn't the same without these tones," Trudel said as she wound and adjusted the hands on the clock. It didn't occur to me that it was only stopped, not broken.

Still amused, Janie made a nod toward to the curtain. The motion was subtle, but I agreed that it might be time to leave.

"Well, we should probably be heading out," I mused out loud for Madame von Hugelstein.

"Yep probably," Janie agreed. She finished her drink and casually slid the empty glass away from her.

Trudel ignored us. She moved down the bar a little and greeted the bust. She straightened up and gently toasted the man with an air of sarcasm. I downed the rest of my drink and took my place behind the bar again. Trudel grimaced at me and returned to the customer side to sit down.

"Ready?" Janie asked in an effort to get us out the door.

"Yes. Madame von Hugelstein," I started. "It was our pleasure …"

The curtain again parted and a new face peered in. Janie and I looked over as my voice trailed off. The man staring back was as silent and expressionless as we were.

"Oh God," Trudel muttered quietly.

The man entered the room. He walked cautiously, as his eyes darted around the bar with a nervous energy. His face was all jowls. Mostly balding, the frumpy man had tried to comb what little hair he had left to cover his entire scalp. The shine on his loafers had long left the shoe, and his sweater vest bore the classic look of a well-laundered article of clothing. I guessed that at one point it had looked expensive.

His round face was framed by large glasses and centered by a well-trimmed little mustache. I looked at Janie, but she was sizing our new company up as well and seemed to have forgotten about the plan to leave for a moment.

"Bonsoir," the man started. He was sweating a little.

"Bonsoir," I answered. "My wife and I are guests here. I actually don't work here or anything. We were just about to leave for dinner …"

"A beer, please," he said.

"Well, uh, okay."

"We might as well, honey," Janie assured me. "I'll have one more, too."

I expected the concierge to step through the curtain at any time to stop the party, but the cloth barrier remained motionless.

"1664 in a bottle, please," he said.

"Of course, sir." I went to the fridge.

He pulled up a stool between the ladies. "Hello, Trudel."

"Hello, Fleuse," she answered, avoiding his gaze. She pronounced it "Flooze."

"You look nice tonight," he offered.

Trudel barely acknowledged this compliment. She raised her eyebrows and huffed softly. She hadn't smiled once until this moment, but she didn't seem to be all that happy.

Fleuse waited for a response, but none came beyond that. He then looked in my direction.

"And who do we have here?" he asked as he looked me up and down.

"My name is Peter. This is my wife, Janie. We are on vacation from Indiana, in the United States."

"I know where Indiana is," he sniffed.

"I'm sorry," I answered, thinking I'd offended the man. "Are you familiar with the United States?"

"I went to New York City one time. I hated it." Again, he turned toward Trudel. He paused, as if weighing his next question. "And how have you been?"

"It hasn't been that long, Fleuse," she answered.

"Well, it's been a little while, at least."

"Maybe."

He glanced nervously back at me to see how intently I was listening or watching. "Maybe," he continued, "we'd be able to have dinner tonight. You know, to catch up a little."

"Fleuse," Trudel said as she authoritatively set her drink on the bar. "I am in love with Victor. It's over."

"Trudel, I am sorry, but Victor is gone. He was my friend, too. I miss him."

"Oh, come off it. You've been waiting for him to disappear just so you could try to win me back."

"That's not true, Trudel."

"Besides, what will you do when he comes back?" she sang out near the top of her voice. "Did you ever think of that? He'll absolutely hate you for this!"

"Comes back? You surely don't believe ..."

Trudel's stare stopped him mid-sentence. It was the first time that she'd actually turned her head to look at him. He slowly swiveled back toward the bar. We rested in silence for a moment, and I again tried to get Janie and me off to dinner.

"Well, it has been nice meeting you both," I started.

Janie was barely listening. She raised her glass to the couple. "Sounds like we need a toast. To Victor, whoever and wherever he may be. I don't know him, but it sounds like he meant a lot to you both. May he come back soon!"

"Here, here," Trudel warbled and took a sip.

Fleuse just sighed. He looked to Janie. "Victor isn't coming back."

Janie looked at me. I shrugged. We both looked back at Fleuse.

"He's dead," he continued.

"I don't believe that!" Trudel exploded. "He is off. Probably with another woman!"

"How could you say that?" Fleuse responded.

"Nothing could kill Victor," she answered wistfully.

"Either way," Fleuse tried again. "Let me take you to dinner!"

"Don't be an idiot!" she exclaimed. "It's over!"

Fleuse retreated to his drink.

Janie looked at me with amusement yet again. As the four of us sipped in silence, it was obvious that we would not be leaving for dinner as soon as I'd hoped.

Chapter III.

A recording of orchestra music sounded its last note in a cramped, dark theatre in the Latin Quarter. A small audience of twenty or so stood and politely clapped in the hot blackness. Trudel von Hugelstein bowed, holding her fellow cast members' sweaty hands.

Trudel knew that this small stage might be the only one she ever would see. Her ambitions included stardom, but she'd been at it her entire life. Fame and fortune would have been a long shot even ten years earlier.

The heavy, rusty stage door creaked as it opened. Blinding daylight in the narrow streets greeted her. Throngs of tourists bustled, searching for cafés and bars, smiling and pointing at awnings further down the way. Trudel pushed herself into the flow of pedestrian traffic.

The seven o'clock performance hadn't opened its doors to an audience yet. She noticed a small line of operagoers as she shuffled passed.

"Excuse me," one woman from the line said as she reached out to her.

"Yes?" Trudel smiled pleasantly, if not genuinely.

"I saw you in this production about a month ago. I loved it."

"Thank you."

"Are you performing this evening?"

"No, no. I just played the matinée today," she answered, reminded that she had failed to win the role for prime showings.

"Aw," the woman uttered sympathetically. "Well, I'm a fan. I wish you were singing tonight."

"Well thank you, dear," Trudel said, forcing a smile.

"When are you singing next? I'm still in town until ..." the woman's voice trailed off.

Trudel was already walking away. Forgetting the woman's slight, the opera singer had begun reminiscing about that day's performance. It was a good show with a nice audience. A small celebration was in order.

She lived just far enough across the river that she never wanted to walk. Yet, it seemed silly to take a taxi such a short distance. This evening, she was happy to stroll. To break the walk into two manageable stretches, she promised herself that she would stop in for a drink at a café.

The area surrounding Place Saint-Michel was crowded. People overran the sidewalks. Even the edges of the fountain were covered with seated youths, flirting and laughing. Trudel couldn't stand youths. She navigated her way to the Quai des Grands-Augustins and set out for her side of the river.

The opera singer knew that most establishments along her way would be swollen with patrons on an early Saturday evening. The pleasant mild air of the summer would turn humid and hot inside a crowded bar. At sidewalk tables, empty glasses and bottles littered white tablecloths, stained with spilled wine. Places like these were not her style.

She wanted quiet. Trudel was hoping to hear the music in her memory. Even as she walked, she was imagining the bright lights that heated her forehead and tore through the blackness above the stage. Before she knew it, she'd lumbered halfway across the river.

Trudel focused her energies toward finding a place to celebrate. She'd recently dated a man who spoke highly of a bar that was near her current path. On the street-level floor of a hotel, this place was unassuming and almost never crowded. While accepting the risk of running into an old flame, she decided to give the Bon Parisien a try.

Slowly striding across the Pont des Arts with her purse swinging majestically at her side, the opera singer could hear the river gently flow beneath her. After a few more turns through the Louvre and a walk down the Avenue de l'Opéra, she finally approached the Hôtel des Bretons. The Bon Parisien's sign beckoned over the corner entrance, warmly lit by a soft buzz. She went inside.

The room itself looked perfect. Not a single item was out of place. She immediately smelled the richness of tobacco and wine vapors sitting heavily in the air. The late afternoon sun warmed the space comfortably like a toaster oven on the lowest setting.

Behind the bar stood a man in his fifties. A little shorter than she, he was grizzled and greyed. Beneath a slightly wrinkled white button up, he was wiry.

The man was alone in the place, and he leaned casually reading a newspaper that he'd laid out on the bar. Nearby, a lone glass of beer rested untouched. He was scowling at whatever it was that he was reading, but the expression quickly disappeared when he looked up to see Trudel walk through the door.

"Good evening, madame," he said, beginning to fold his paper.

"Good evening," Trudel answered as she headed for a table near the bar, exhausted by the walk.

"Please have a seat. What may I serve you?" the man asked, hurrying out to meet her. He pulled a chair out from an empty table for her.

"Not too busy tonight, no?" she asked as she took the seat, failing to thank the man.

"There have been a few to come and go."

"Is someone waiting for that drink?" she asked, nodding to the glass on the bar.

"No, it's mine. I'm celebrating."

"Oh, congratulations. What are you celebrating?"

"Well, it's a long story, but this," the man said with a grand gesture around the Bon Parisien.

"I don't understand."

"It's my one week anniversary working here."

"Oh. Good for you," she answered. "What luck. I've found a bartender in training."

"Don't worry, madame," he responded, smiling. He spoke plainly and softly. "I think you'll find that I can get you anything you need. I'll be your personal barkeep."

Trudel found the man charming. The opera singer felt slightly disarmed.

"Oh well, congratulations indeed," she answered pleasantly, regretting her earlier sarcasm.

"And what may I get you tonight? We do have some nice wines just in."

"Let's see, I guess that I could drink a glass of wine. I too am celebrating."

"Excellent! Do you have a favorite?"

"Red. A Medoc if you have it."

"I do," he answered, scurrying back to the bar. "What is your occasion this evening?"

"I have just finished a grand performance this afternoon. I sing. I am in an opera."

"How interesting." He painstakingly uncorked the bottle of Medoc. "Where is your production?"

"On the left bank. We have a nice little cast. They do well, but I have had to guide them through some of the harder times in rehearsals. They are not as experienced as I am."

"Very good," he said. "My name is Victor. Victor Laquer."

"Trudel von Hugelstein."

"Trudel von Hugelstein," he repeated, smiling pleasantly. "The opera star."

She blushed and smiled coyly.

"May I sit with you while no one's here?" he asked, arriving with her drink.

*   *   *

"... So, just one second before I hit the final, climactic note," Trudel said, several drinks later, "the power goes out."

"Oh no," Victor answered.

She had been recounting one of her favorite experiences, and Victor seemed to be enjoying it. A quiet couple whispered a few tables away and a group of four men laughed and drank near the front door. Victor had been pulled away more than once but stayed with the opera singer otherwise.

"Truly," the opera singer added, "it was total darkness. Plus, the music had stopped."

"So what did you do?"

"Well, I almost panicked."

"I would guess!"

"But, I'm a professional. I didn't let it get the best of me. I took a big deep breath, and I hit that last note like it was the last note I'd ever sing."

"In the dark? Brilliant!" Victor said, smiling.

"It was," she laughed as she sipped her drink. "The audience loved it. They thought it was on purpose."

"Really?"

"Yes. They thought the lights went out for dramatic effect."

"That's incredible," the bartender marveled.

"It was great," Trudel said still chuckling, almost hearing the applause.

"You must be quite an entertainer."

"Sadly," she conceded, "the ushers had to escort everyone out of the theater with flashlights. I thought that undermined the effect."

They each took a drink. Another patron entered from the street, and Victor rose to greet him. Trudel watched Victor prepare a drink for him, chatting pleasantly as he worked. For a brief moment, Victor put on a set of wire-rimmed glasses to read the label of a wine bottle. Trudel found him attractive. He looked almost academic for a moment.

After serving the man, Victor returned to their table.

"Sorry for the distraction," he said to Trudel, folding his glasses and placing them in the breast pocket of his shirt.

"I like those," the opera singer said, nodding to the eyewear.

"Well, I don't," he answered, smiling. "I used them more often at my former job."

"You seem like an excellent bartender. What did you do before this?"

"I was an accountant until recently."

"Really? Numbers?"

"Yes," Victor nodded. "I've worked for many firms in my career."

"Interesting," Trudel said. "So what brings you here? Are you retired?"

Victor shifted in his seat. "No, not exactly. I was recently let go."

"Oh, I'm sorry to hear that."

"We don't have to get into it," the bartender answered. For the first time in the evening, he wasn't smiling or flirting. "The partners at the firm were terrible. They never listened to me. I'm sure they'll run themselves out of business any day now."

He frowned into his drink as he took another sip.

"So, how about you?" he asked, returning to his cordial tone. "I was an accountant, now a bartender. You are an opera singer and a ...?" His voice trailed off, leading her.

"That's it."

"That's it?" he asked as he raised his eyebrows.

"Yes."

"You must be quite good, then."

"Well yes, I've been doing this a long time."

"You are in high demand then, no? How often do you perform?"

"Sometimes up to six nights a week," she lied, liking Victor's opinion of her so far. It had been years since she'd actually worked that often.

"That's fantastic."

"Well," she conceded. "I do have a little family money."

"That always helps. It must have been substantial."

"Why would you guess that?"

"Well, as a former accountant, I know money. I'm guessing that you've never been married then?"

"I have not been. How did you know?"

"I assume you are a little younger than I am," he said.

She blushed.

He continued, "Most people in our generation don't refer to it as 'family money' anymore if they have shared it with a husband, had to split it in a divorce, funded a child's education, etc."

"You are correct. I have never been married."

"Are you from Paris originally?" he continued.

"I am. I was born here."

"I could tell."

"Really?!" She blushed again. "How can you tell?"

"I don't know," he shrugged, smiling.

"My mother was French. She met my father in Paris. He was a German soldier, unfortunately stationed here during the occupation."

"Goodness," Victor said almost absent-mindedly. The table of men in the room was starting to get a little loud. They were beginning to distract Victor, annoying him. He made sure to keep listening to Trudel despite the noise.

"My father," Trudel continued without noticing, "managed to escape prosecution after the liberation. My mother instinctively hated the Nazis, but she could not help herself with my father. She was in love."

"My, that is compelling. It's a classic example of love conquering all," Victor added, spying the rowdy table out of the corner of his eye.

"I was born during the war, but their story is sad beyond that. As a child, I lived publicly as the daughter of the enemy. Luckily, I had a beautiful voice and a sweet personality. I was able to win over my educators, neighbors, and friends."

"Well, you are innately French. I don't think you feel like an enemy."

"That's good," she chuckled.

"So what happened to your father? How did he escape prosecution? That would have been a feat, no?"

"He remained in Paris with my mother and me for a few years. He wasn't able to stay long. Our community knew who he was. He wasn't embraced. I'd say he was more tolerated. But, they knew that we were a family, and the authorities never came looking for him. He was just a private in the German army."

"If you don't mind me asking, do you know where he went? You don't have to answer if you wouldn't like to."

"No it's fine. I have no idea where he went. For all I know, he was thrown in jail after he left. Who knows?"

"Did you get a chance to say goodbye?"

"Truthfully, I don't remember him saying goodbye. I don't really remember too much at all anyway. Everything I know is from what my mother has told me."

Suddenly, a glass shattered in the bar. Victor's head snapped up in time to see the loud table of men in the bar erupt with laughter. One of the patrons had dropped his drink, and there were shards of glass everywhere in the vicinity of the table. Trudel saw Victor turn red.

"Excuse me," he said through his teeth. Victor jumped up with an impressive speed and purpose. "Gentlemen!" he shouted.

They immediately were silenced.

"I will not tolerate such behavior in this bar!" he thundered as he approached the table.

Trudel was silently impressed with him.

"Sorry, monsieur!" one of the men began.

Not listening, Victor snagged a fistful of one of the men's sweaters and pulled him toward the door, his fingernails raking the skin beneath. Pulling the man clear out of his chair, Victor yelled, "This is a place of class!"

The unruly patron stumbled behind him, knocking over a chair in the process. The rest of the men at the table leapt after their friend, drunkenly whooping and laughing. Upon reaching the door, Victor heaved the man on to the sidewalk outside. The other three ran passed the bartender to join their friend. One turned as the door was closing.

"So sorry for him!" he yelled. "We haven't paid yet!"

Victor had already turned back for the bar but wheeled upon hearing the man's voice. Still red-faced and huffing from the one-sided skirmish, he yelled, "It's on the house! You can repay me by never coming back in here again!"

The group helped their friend off the sidewalk and disappeared into the soft evening light. Victor returned to Trudel's table.

"I'm sorry about that," he said to Trudel without sitting. "Another drink?"

"Yes, thank you."

He went to work opening another bottle of wine.

"My, that was something," she marveled as the bartender worked. "You are a bruiser!"

Victor smiled.

"Does that happen often?" she continued.

"I don't know," he said from behind the bar. "Still my first week."

The opera singer lifted her eyebrows. "Rough for an accountant."

He smirked and nodded toward the wine. "Well, I hope you'll let me buy this one for you."

"I won't say no."

A moment passed as Trudel continued to ruminate on the events of the last few moments. She heard Victor exhale, suggesting he was shaking off the encounter.

"Well, we were speaking about family," he said, returning to the table. "Are you close with yours? Or I should ask, do you have any anymore?"

"No, I am all alone." In truth, she didn't feel at all alone in that moment.

*   *   *

The couple had been through better than two bottles of wine. Once again alone, their tabletop was littered with stained coasters and small drops of spilled wine. With complete darkness having overtaken the windows, Trudel was out later than she'd been in a long time. Remarkably, she hadn't even thought about the performance earlier in the day.

"I, too, am Parisian," Victor started in. "I have been an accountant all my life."

"Are those related to one another?"

He laughed. "I guess not. I don't know why I said it like that."

"So, how did you get this job?" Trudel asked.

"I've been in here a few times. I live a few neighborhoods away. After I lost my job, I inquired for a few days at other accounting firms. Without luck there, I came in here. I figured it might be a nice change of pace, and they hired me on the spot."

Trudel looked around the room. "It seems like a comfortable place."

"It is. Now I just need traffic to pick up a little," he said as he tidied up his side of the table.

"Does the hotel have many guests?"

"If they do, I haven't seen a lot of them over the last week."

"Do you ever go out to listen to music?" she asked.

"I have not done too much of that. Is that something I should be embarrassed to admit to a fine musician such as yourself?"

"Well, we can change that. Would you be interested in seeing an opera?"

Victor temporarily re-corked their third wine bottle and set it aside. "I would," he said simply.

She took a sip and enjoyed the moment but wasn't courageous enough to let it sit too long. "I really like this place."

"How did you wind up here today?"

"I just decided to pop in somewhere on my way home."

"So you must live close?"

"I do, just on Rue Thérèse."

"Oh, that's not far," he said, sipping wine through purple lips. "So, you just looked in and decided this was the spot?"

"No. It came recommended."

"Oh! Well, that's great. By whom?"

"By a man. He was a man I used to date."

"He recommended the place but never brought you here?"

"We weren't together long."

"I see. Well, what's his name? Maybe I met him this week."

"We didn't hit it off. He was much more interested in me than I was in him."

"Don't you just hate that? Happens to me too all the time," Victor joked.

"Yes?" Trudel answered smiling.

"Oh yes, I've been hit on all week. I just say, 'Listen, I work here. What you see is not for sale.'"

Trudel laughed.

"So, who is it?" Victor persisted.

"His name is Fleuse Newman."

"Really? Fleuse?" he asked with surprise.

"Yes, do you know him?"

"Well, I do."

"He is a regular in here?"

"Well, I don't know about that, but he says he drops in every now and then. We have known each other for many years. I have handled the finances for his clock business for some time now."

"He does make beautiful pieces."

"Yes he does," Victor said with a smile. "Small world."

"But, we were not right for each other. It was good that it ended."

"I'll have to tell him that I ran into you the next time I see him."

"Don't go out of your way. Truly, it's better this way."

"I see."

"Anyway, I'm glad he didn't bring me here," Trudel said, smiling. "Now it is mine."

Chapter IV.

I sipped whiskey. Oaky vapors stung my nose inside the glass. Fleuse and Trudel sat at a table, speaking quietly. He leaned in and trained his gaze on her. She sat facing away from him, making a point not to look him in the eye.

I was still standing behind the bar, feeling good. The coolness of a damp bar rag numbed my shoulder. Keeping meticulous track of our expenses on the job, Janie and I had just finished stuffing the money for another round into the envelope. She sat on one of the bar stools facing me and was trying her best to make it appear as if she were not listening to the two at a table behind her.

"I guess dinner's off for a while," I shrugged, tucking the envelope alongside the register.

"Are you kidding?" she whispered. "We're right in the middle of high drama over here. I'm not even thinking about dinner anymore."

"I was really looking forward to a little something to eat."

"Me too, honey. We'll go in a bit, but think about the story that this will make later on. You can't make this stuff up."

"You have a point."

"Damn straight, muffin," she jabbed with a smile. "I always have a point."

I tilted my head back and exhaled. Twenties-era parlor tiles covered the ceiling.

"God, this place is beautiful. I still can't believe they even let us come in here," I mused.

"I know."

"I mean, how often is it that you get to come to Paris and actually run a bar?"

"Shhh. Focus. I'm trying to listen here," she whispered, taking another sip. Nodding toward Fleuse and Trudel, she added, "Do you think she's going to give him another shot?"

"I don't know. Probably not."

"You can tell he wants it really badly."

"She's too in love with the old bartender," I said doubtfully.

"Victor?"

"That's him."

We both took a drink.

"So what do you think?" I continued. "Is the old guy dead or has he run off with another woman?"

"Who knows?"

"What does this guy here see in her, anyway?" I asked Janie.

"I don't know. I think she's kind of cool."

"Are you serious?"

"Yeah. She's in an opera. A bona fide diva."

"I think she's just bossy."

"That's because she doesn't really like you. She's a grand dame of France," Janie said, smiling.

"Well, what makes you think she likes you any better? You're an American, too."

"Nah. We're friends."

I scoffed quietly. "What makes you think that?"

"We got each others' backs," Janie said with a look over toward Trudel. "I can just tell."

"Please," I winced.

As I took another sip of my drink, I noticed Fleuse place his hand on Trudel's as they were talking. She ripped it away from him rapidly and chirped harshly under her breath. He immediately diverted his gaze in submission.

"Classic case of boy meets girl, girl doesn't care," Janie mused softly.

"Kind of reminds me of us in the beginning," I suggested.

"What? No. I never treated you like this," Janie protested.

"Well, true. But you made me work for it a little, you have to admit."

"I did not."

I made a face. "You backed away the first time I tried to kiss you."

"All part of my master plan," she said with a sip.

"C'mon. You didn't know what you were doing."

"If we'd kissed on the first night we met, we would have ruined it all" she said, still trying to listen to our guests at the table. "You should be glad I backed away. You weren't ready for me. We never would have found ourselves here."

"Please."

"Don't stare," she warned. "They are going to think you're super creepy."

"They haven't seen me."

"Are you kidding? You couldn't be more obvious."

"I just don't get it," I said as I drained my drink. "How is he attracted to her? She isn't exactly pretty."

"Hey take it easy. Don't be a jerk," she snapped quietly.

"I just don't see it, that's all."

"Look at him too, honey," Janie rationalized. "That guy isn't exactly a model himself or anything."

"True."

"He's like a turtle-man," she said as she tilted her head.

"Well, she's kind of a hippo in a fur coat. Maybe they were good for each other."

"We're mean," she said, laughing quietly.

"I wasn't like this before I met you. What did you do to me?" I mused.

"Sure you weren't," she snickered.

Once again, the curtain whipped to one side. All the heads in the room turned. A short, thin man stepped proudly through the opening. He wore a ratty tweed suit, and his straight hair was parted inexactly across his head. Still expecting to leave soon to make a night of dinner and exploring the streets of Paris, I felt something inside me sink as the man entered.

"Mes amis!" he exclaimed as he looked at the four of us.

Fleuse righted in his seat. I thought I could detect a mild eye-roll, but it wasn't obvious. He likely didn't appreciate any interruption to his alone time with Trudel.

"I am sorry, sir," I greeted him, hoping to squash any conversation or bar request before it happened. "We are not open tonight. All of us were just getting ready to shut down ..."

"Fleuse, my dear. How are you?" the short man ignored me as he advanced into the room. "Why does it always smell like a library in here?"

Fleuse stood up part way. "Jacques, hello. Just happened to be in the neighborhood, eh?" he asked unenthusiastically.

"As a matter of fact, yes. What are the chances I'd run into you?"

Fleuse didn't smile. "Pretty good, I'm guessing."

"I see you've brought a lady!"

"He didn't bring me," Trudel snapped.

"Have you ever met Trudel von Hugelstein?" Fleuse asked.

"Madame von Hugelstein!" Jacques sung. "I am Jacques Pistache, the renowned and celebrated street performer."

"Hello," she said cautiously. I could see her sizing him up.

"Nice try, honey," Janie whispered to me with a smile. She swayed slightly as she leaned toward me across the bar. "Looks like we'll be good-timing here a little while longer."

"And," Pistache said, turning in our direction, "who do we have here?"

"A couple of Americans," Trudel announced.

"Hello," I began. "My name is Peter. This is my wife, Janie. We are on holiday."

"My, my, my. Hello Janie, ma cherie," the renowned and celebrated street performer replied with wide eyes.

"Nice to meet you," Janie said somewhat amused. "You said it was Jacques ... Peest-ahsh?"

"You are a beautiful creature," the man pushed forward without confirming Janie's pronunciation.

"Ok, ok," I jumped in, unable to suppress my smirk. "Take it easy."

"I rarely have an occasion to see real beauty up close," he said, never taking his eyes off Janie.

"Stop it," she said as she lifted a hand in his direction.

"May I get you a drink?" I asked, trying my best to appear cool with someone so blatantly hitting on my wife.

"A beer, young man," he said.

"Easy. I can get a quick one for you." I turned for a glass. I was still hoping to find a way to rush him out without being rude. "So what brings you in tonight?"

"Oh, I was in the neighborhood," he confirmed again as he pulled a stool up next to Janie.

"Give it up, honey," Janie softly whispered. "We might be in for a while longer."

I nodded, feeling the tenor of the evening moving in that direction. She wasn't suggesting we stay because she liked him. In fact, she scooted her chair a little farther from him when he made the move to sit down. Nonetheless, Janie was being entertained. Like me, she wanted dinner. But clearly, she was enjoying the bar experience at the Bon Parisien too much to want to leave.

"You said you're a street performer?" I asked Pistache as I poured his beer. "What do you do?"

"Well, I'm glad you asked," he replied happily. "I have been known to do a little dancing and a little magic." With this, he did a little tap dance on the crossbar of the stool and produced a single playing card from behind Janie's ear.

"Look at this card, my dear, and don't tell me what it is," he crowed.

"Okay. Um … why? I don't see the rest of the deck anywhere," she responded.

"Because it's the ace of spades!" he exclaimed and waited for applause. No one reacted. Janie just looked at the card.

"Did I get it right?" he asked.

"Yeah," she answered, unable to take him seriously.

"Of course you did," I interrupted and smiled.

"Well, how was I supposed to know what card she had hidden behind her ear?!" Pistache exclaimed.

"It was in your hand the whole time!" I replied humorlessly.

"Relax. Don't take it too seriously. That's the point of the joke," he softly clarified.

"Ah I see," I said.

"I get it now. You do comedy too," Janie said.

"That I do. What did the snail say to the snake?"

"I don't know," she answered.

"For a slitherer, you're so slow that I can sew a boa in the time it takes you to say 'ssssss.'"

No one laughed. I scratched my head as I tried to work out the French to English translation in my head.

"I think I get it," Janie said, as she looked at me and shrugged.

"It wasn't that funny," I heard Fleuse mutter.

"Not at all," Trudel snorted into her drink.

"No, it is funny!" Pistache explained. "Because snails can't sew. And they're slow. And he's sewing a boa. Which is a snake."

I smiled more at him than with him. At least he was entertaining.

"It's poetic. Wordplay. I get it," Janie said.

"You're into that sort of thing?!" Pistache exclaimed.

"She studies poetry, and writes it," I stated. "Really good, too."

Janie smiled modestly. "Okay, that's enough."

"Excellent! So you do get it!" Pistache said confidently. "The rest of you are crazy if you don't think that's pure comedy gold."

"Okay, we're crazy," Trudel declared.

He ignored her. "Also, I can sing a little, and execute perfect impressions of the stars!"

"Huh," I mulled it over. "Who can you impersonate?"

"Well, an impression is not the same as an impersonation."

"Oh, okay. What is the difference?"

"In an impersonation, you act like someone else. You try to get their mannerisms down."

"Got it, yes."

"A impression is a vocal imprint."

"What's that mean?" I asked.

"You take a mold in your mind of their vocal patterns: the tones, the inflection, the pitch. Then, you form your vocal chords in a way to replicate the sound of their voice."

"Isn't an impression part of an impersonation?" I asked as I made another drink for myself.

"Don't be stupid, American," Pistache snapped.

"Huh," Trudel grunted. "That sounds like nothing to me."

"Nothing? I have entertained audiences here and in Italy and Spain!"

"On the street?" Trudel jabbed.

"That is my best medium!" Jacques exclaimed with a swig and a wink at Janie. If Trudel's tone was wearing thin on him, it didn't seem to register.

"Well, let's see it," I urged. "Do you do anyone I know?"

"Of course! Are you familiar with legendary French royal Marie Antoinette?"

"Yes. You can do an impersonation of her?" I asked.

"Impression," he corrected me.

"How do you even know what her voice sounded like?" Trudel challenged.

"I've heard of her, but I'm not very familiar with her," I added.

"I can see that you are going to need an American celebrity, aren't you?" Pistache continued, ignoring the opera singer.

"Probably," I admitted.

"These two," he grunted playfully as he thumbed in our direction. "Okay let's have it, then. Who do you want?"

"Just pick an impersonation you like to do," Janie chimed in.

"Impression," he corrected her.

"Right, sorry," she said with a raised eyebrow.

"How about the greatest pop singer of all time, Frank Sinatra!?" Pistache sang.

"Yes, perfect," I said.

Jacques lowered his chin and cleared this throat a few times. His eyes bulged. Awkwardly moving his mouth as if adjusting for extra teeth, he finally settled in on a bizarre look somewhere between mid-ranged angst and a complete muscular crimping of the face. Janie looked my way and smiled.

"Hey, Dean-O!" Pistache began in English with a horrific accent. It was closer to a slurring Bostonian than Ol' Blue Eyes. "Roll me a seven and we all end up winn-ahs!"

I couldn't keep from giggling a little, burying my face in a sip of drink to avoid betrayal. It seemed as though he took his craft very seriously.

"Hey, Sammy!" he continued spitting words with wide eyes. "Kick it ah-ff! I'll show you a real fahx-trot if you get me an-ah-thah highball!"

"Okay, I think we get the picture," I said unable to contain my laughter. Janie was right with me.

Fleuse stared into his beer as he ignored him. Trudel seemed horrified by this person's definition of talent.

Pistache snapped out of it. "See? Exactly right, no?"

"Sure," I said.

"Is that what you did on streets in Italy and Spain?" Trudel spat.

"Well, I also did a little tap dancing."

"Didn't we see a little of that already?" Trudel asked disdainfully.

"Here's another little taste just for you, madame," he said still oblivious to her tone. A slight shuffle of his feet again on the crossbar of his barstool preceded a series of disorganized taps during which he lost his balance, reached for the bar to catch himself, and knocked over his own beer. Everyone began laughing.

"That usually doesn't happen," Pistache sheepishly said while smiling at himself. He immediately grabbed his beer in an attempt to salvage whatever was left. I also went to the rescue with my bar rag.

"I usually don't fall down," he continued. He looked at Janie. "But, I'm sure you would have had me if I'd fallen all the way, right?"

"Sure, man," Janie said in English.

"I knew I could count on you, ma cherie," he said with a sly smile.

"C'mon," I said. "Seriously, that's enough man."

"You call yourself a renowned performer?" Trudel challenged as she stood. "I would like to know. What does that mean? Who heralds your talents?"

"What do you mean by that?" Pistache retorted, finally dropping the act for the first time.

"I mean that I am Trudel von Hugelstein."

"So?"

"You haven't heard of me?"

After a brief moment, Pistache brightened. "Wait, you're Victor's Trudie!"

Fleuse shifted in his seat.

"Well yes, I am that," she said. "But that's not what I mean. Surely, you have seen me upon the stage or heard about my voice."

"I think I'd heard that Victor was seeing a singer maybe, yes!"

"Well, I have performed quite a lot through the years. I thought maybe a fellow performer like you would have been aware of the other acts in the neighborhood."

"Well, I travel around a bit. I'm sorry."

"That's not important," Trudel grunted. "I haven't heard of you. Based on what I've seen here, I'm not surprised. What makes you 'renowned,' as you say?"

"I have a few awards for local entertainment," he defended himself with a little more vigor. "I do not believe that I need to justify myself to you."

"What awards?"

"The key to the city of Antony."

Fleuse leaned back in his chair and huffed.

"Congratulations," Trudel drove on sarcastically. "It's just that my talent is a gift. Furthermore, I have worked to perfect and hone that gift for many years. And now, I must share ranks with this!" she exclaimed to the room while motioning toward Pistache.

"Trudel, honey," Fleuse tried.

"I'm not your 'honey,' Fleuse!" Trudel spat with fire as she wheeled to address him.

Pistache turned to me. "I get this a lot. Others get jealous of my talents."

Trudel choked on the last sip of her drink.

"Yep, I understand," I humored him. Attempting to steer the group away from more of this talk, I looked to Fleuse. "How do you two know each other?"

They exchanged a glance.

"We go way back," Pistache said contently.

"We are friends," Fleuse said, obviously dodging the question.

"Every now and then we work together," Pistache said with a smile.

"Do you hire him to do impersonations at parties?" I asked Fleuse with a grin.

"Impressions," Pistache corrected.

"Yeah, right."

"No," Fleuse said humorlessly. Apparently he didn't think too much of Pistache's talents either.

"I actually sell secondhand jewelry as well. He uses me as a supplier for metals and stones, really," Pistache added.

"There it is," Trudel said with a sly smile. "I knew it. A day job."

"A salesman," Janie commented. "Makes perfect sense."

"Not my day job," Pistache interjected defensively. "It's more like a side job."

Trudel had already looked away. She'd stopped listening. I looked at Fleuse, who didn't seem to care to jump in either.

Noticing my glass feeling light, I asked, "Okay. Who's ready for another drink?"

Chapter V.

Outside the window of the clockmaker's shop, a rainy Paris bustled. Anyone passing by could have caught a glimpse of Fleuse Newman, but they'd have to look carefully.

From the exterior, the shop looked dark and locked up. But a look through the blackened, wet, and fogged windows would reveal the warm glow of Fleuse's cramped workspace toward the back of the shop, with the man huddled in the halo of his worklight.

From the inside, drops of water obscured the view of the street. Shapes passed back and forth in front of the window like an impressionist painting in motion. The greyness of the sky kept the corners of the place slightly darker than usual. With heavy, humid air, the room smelled like wet wood.

The small, one-room shop was crowded with clock faces, gears, pendulums, and thousands of other tiny parts. The chorus of ticks and tocks that filled the room could have driven the clockmaker to insanity. So could have the small wooden work stool or the heat from the lamp hung casually on the end of a skeletal steel arm directly above him. But, none of it bothered Fleuse.

He hovered over his work as still as if he were being photographed. His projects were of such an intricate nature that he had to be practically frozen to complete them. His face was adorned with a contorted look of deep concentration. He nearly had to remind himself to blink. At a glance, one wouldn't have been able to see him breathe.

The only motion that existed was miniscule and usually at the tips of his fingers. When he shifted in his seat or reached for a new tool, his muscles tightened and twisted as if he'd been asleep for hours. Fleuse wasn't uncomfortable, though. The clockmaker was happiest when staring through the magnifying double lens loupe attached to the frame of his glasses. That is how he preferred to see the world: one tiny space at a time.

Fleuse existed in this manner for many years. He was the middle child in a family of five. He was the only one of his parents' children to show any interest in his father's clock-making business, so he naturally took it over as a young man. It was the only career he'd ever known.

The ring of the front entrance broke the clockmaker's concentration. Fleuse looked up to see a portly young man making his way through the narrow paths of works in progress. Newman removed his glasses, more than slightly disappointed with the interruption.

"Bonjour," Fleuse greeted, trying to sound a little cordial.

"Oh, bonjour," coughed the man.

"Is there something that I can help you find?"

"No, no," the young man exclaimed. "I was just walking by and became intrigued with your collection. My grandfather had one just like this one here." He motioned toward a half-finished clock with several components laid out in front of it.

"Well, as you can see, that is not quite completed."

"Yes, yes," the man said. "The face and the numbers look almost exactly the same though."

"Excellent," Fleuse said, hoping the man would leave.

After an awkward moment or two, the man asked, "How much is it?"

"Um," Fleuse stammered. "That particular one is not for sale."

"Not for sale?"

"I mean, it's already been sold," he lied. Like all his works, he built clocks for a specific type of customer. This man was slovenly and didn't fit the profile. He would rather have seen the timepiece in the hands of someone more likely to keep it clean and well maintained.

"Oh, okay. It's a shame. I like it!" The man laughed nervously. Another unfinished piece caught his eye. "Quite the showroom you have here."

"It's really more of a workspace."

"I see that. How do you keep track of everything?"

Fleuse shrugged. "I don't know."

After a few more awkward moments, the man asked, "Do you actually have anything for sale in here?"

Fleuse looked around. "Um," he stammered.

Sensing a dead end, the man said, "Don't worry about it. I really need to be going anyway. Thanks for your time."

After hearing the door shut behind the visitor, Fleuse heavily exhaled. He didn't like speaking to people he didn't know. Most of his customers were referrals or commissions. If he could legally weld the front door shut, he would.

The clockmaker retreated to his workbench and settled in on a timepiece of a new design. Suspended above his work, he carefully set the two hands of the clock in front of him. Opening a drawer in his workbench, he fished out a small box that rattled when he touched it. He removed the small lid, and carefully pinched one of several very small diamonds between his thumb and index fingers.

Working with a surgeon's precision, Fleuse began the painstaking but rewarding task of setting the diamonds into the hands of the clock. Although his clocks did not always include jewels, Fleuse had worked hard to maintain a working knowledge of precious stones and metals. He found that it helped set his work apart. Without any formal training as a jeweler, it had taken Fleuse years to know how to handle something with the delicate beauty of a diamond.

*   *   *

Less than an hour later, the tiny bell above his door again rang as the door opened. Fleuse felt the blood rush to his head at the thought of another guest, but his friend Jacques Pistache sauntered through the doorway.

"Fleuse! Mon ami!" Jacques exclaimed loudly. He was carrying a small wooden box with him.

"Jacques, good morning. How are you?"

"Last night, my friend. Last night," Pistache announced with some pomp.

"Yes?"

"Everything glowed. This party was perhaps the nicest I've ever seen. So many beautiful women. Chandeliers and champagne. The dance floor didn't have a spare inch. You would have loved it!" Jacques swayed as he still heard the music.

"Sounds like I would have hated it."

"Yes, you are probably right. I loved it. Someday it may be me. You never know."

"I've never been to anything like that."

Jacques snapped out of it and absentmindedly eyed Fleuse's inventory. "Well, the crowds aside, I bet you would have enjoyed it. I fully expected to see a celebrity or royalty enter at any moment."

"Stop touching the clocks. Those woods have just this morning been polished. Shipping off today."

"Sorry."

"So, celebrities you said? Were you able to meet anyone interesting?"

"I did in fact!" Jacques exclaimed. "There was the most ridiculous couple."

Fleuse smirked. He thought that they were probably normal people.

"Let me tell you," Pistache continued. "The seafood spread. It was incredible."

"I don't like seafood."

"I know. But, you would have been impressed at the sight of it alone, I'm guessing."

"I'm allergic."

"You are not, take it easy."

"I tell people I am," Fleuse said.

"How can you? I thought you were allergic to them, too."

Fleuse finally smiled.

"And the room," Pistache continued. "It was bright. There were chandeliers. It was the life."

"You said something about them already. You're dreaming, Jacques."

"Maybe. But it's all out there for the taking."

"Okay enough about the party."

"Yes. Down to business!" Jacques segued. "I have brought some nice pieces for you." He opened his box. "Here is a nice necklace. I have several rings today. Some traditional yellow gold, a few white gold. One diamond earring. As usual, all available upon consignment."

"I can work with some of these metals. The diamond in this earring will definitely be useful," the clockmaker said as he perused the selection in the box.

"You know what always gets me about parties like that one?" Pistache mused.

"What?" Fleuse asked.

"I feel as though the host doesn't know anyone there."

"Probably not. You're right."

"If you were going to throw a party, wouldn't you want to have all your friends there?"

"Well when you are people as wealthy as it sounds like your host was last night, their friends bring friends, who in turn bring friends."

"I guess I just don't know enough people," Pistache lamented.

"Since it seems that all you can talk about is being rich," Fleuse said while still examining the merchandise, "let's discuss a price."

"Wait. Here's one last thing. I have this."

Pistache dug deep into his pocket and produced a coin. It was about an inch and a half diameter. The metal was well worn and no longer shining, but it was very clean. A man's profile was minted on one side, but a large scratch obscured the details.

Fleuse's face scrunched up. He put his glasses on, took the coin, and examined it thoroughly under his lamp. "It looks old," he observed. "If it has a date, I can't read it."

"I figured that much."

"Where did it come from?"

"Same as everything else," Pistache said.

"It's damaged. See this large scar pattern from something?"

"Yes. Do you think it will affect the value?"

"Absolutely. How much do you want for the whole lot of it?" Fleuse asked.

"Oh, I don't know. What do you think?"

"Don't give me all that, Jacques. You know exactly how much you expect to get from all of this."

"I know what I'm hoping to get, that's for sure. Don't worry though, Fleuse my dear. I trust you completely to begin working with all of this."

Fleuse made a disapproving sound.

"You're waiting because you don't know how much the coin is worth, aren't you?" Fleuse guessed.

"You got me. Everything else I have figured out."

"Even the earring? Stones can be tricky."

"Even the earring," Pistache answered. "I'll be honest about it. It's not as nice as I'd hoped when I got it, but I know the details now on it nonetheless. I can be fair about it. The only thing I was not sure how to price was the coin here."

"Yes, me neither. I don't even recognize the face."

"I expected you to at least be able to do that," Pistache remarked.

"Why would I be able to do that?"

"You would think a guy like you would know stuff about history or something."

"Why would I know about history?"

"I don't know. Maybe because you never go anywhere. You probably watch documentaries or read or something."

"Even if I knew the face, it might not matter. There is a sizeable flaw directly across the front of the coin." Fleuse studied it for a few more silent moments.

"Okay, how about three thousand euros for everything except the coin. We'll sort that one out when we get more information on it."

"Yes, sounds good," Fleuse said without looking up from the object. "I really wish there was a date on this."

"I really feel that it is very old. But, I don't know the first thing about coins. Do you think it's worth anything at all?"

"Might be."

"I suppose that you can always melt it down," Jacques suggested.

"You're right. I guess I could regain the original shine if I melted it and buffed it.

"Maybe we should do that."

"I would need to know first if it is pure. It could easily be a colored iron or something. That wouldn't be much use to us."

"I hadn't considered that."

"Either way, I'd hate to do that before we know how much it was worth in its current state."

"So how do we do that?" Pistache asked.

"I don't really know. It should be worth at least a little something," Fleuse mumbled, still inspecting it. "I do have a friend, though."

"A friend?"

"Well, more of a colleague with whom I'm friendly," Fleuse said slowly as he allowed himself to be distracted by the coin's features.

"Okay. Do you mean that they are an appraiser or something?"

"Or something. It's just someone who knows old currency. Happens to be a coin collector in his spare time. Maybe he'll be able to tell us about it."

Chapter VI.

Now deep into the dizzy of a few drinks, I plunked out a melody at the piano. The old ivory keys were cracked and dirty. The instrument was out of tune as well. Janie sat with me, jotting verse on to a napkin.

Behind me, Fleuse and Trudel were still at their table. Pistache slowly swayed along with the piano. Although he was the most recent addition, he'd already managed more booze than anyone.

"Okay, that's enough of that!" Trudel shouted at me from her spot at the table.

"Let him play!" Pistache slurred dreamily.

"I just finished my drink, and I need another. What kind of bartender are you?" The opera singer shrieked.

"The tourist kind," I laughed and looked at Janie.

"Honey, get her a drink," she urged under her breath.

I stood, abruptly stopping the music. We walked back to the bar.

"Aww," Pistache groaned. "What shall I dance to now?" The part in his hair was beginning to give way and send dark strands flopping over his face.

"I didn't come to my favorite bar in the world tonight not to drink anything," Trudel lamented. "Here it's been closed for a few weeks and this is what I have to return to."

"He is doing his best," Fleuse backed me up. "It's better than serving ourselves."

"Is it?!" she barked.

Pistache had a mischievous look about him. He fired out at Trudel, "If you can tell me how to make something as simple as a martini, then I will buy your next drink."

"Go to hell," she shot back.

"That's what I thought. You couldn't serve yourself if you tried."

"Okay everyone," I began to diffuse the conversation. "What is the next round?"

"How about another Esprit de la Nuit?" Janie mused.

"What's that?" Trudel asked.

"It's a drink we made up before you arrived," I answered. "Would you like to try it?"

"I'll hate it," the opera singer answered. "I'll stick with another whiskey, neat."

"Oh, I think I could take another beer," Pistache slurred.

"A beer please," said Fleuse.

"Here's an idea," Pistache practically jumped in the air. "We should play a drinking game!"

"We're listening," Janie answered. She smiled at me. We have a good time with drinking games with our friends.

Trudel rolled her eyes, but Fleuse nodded.

"Well, I'm thinking maybe something that says 'welcome to Europe' for the both of you," Pistache continued. "Perhaps something that involves the loss of clothing." He couldn't resist gauging Janie's reaction out of the corner of his eye.

"No," both Janie and I definitively reacted. She sighed and shook her head at me. However, Fleuse missed our exchange as he eagerly looked toward Trudel, who rolled her eyes and made a "pfft" sound.

"Okay then, new idea." Pistache recovered. "Does anyone have a deck of cards? I assure you, all clothes will stay on."

"I do, upstairs in my bag," Janie offered.

"Victor always kept some back there somewhere," Fleuse said. He stood and approached the bar top. Leaning in, he squinted over the top of his glasses at the area behind me. "Try that cupboard down there."

I turned, squatted, and found nothing besides a few cobwebs and some dirty glassware. "I don't see it."

"It is probably in a shoebox. I think it was blue. Try the cupboard next to that one."

I moved over one and the search continued.

"Should be a deck of cards ... some dice?" His speech was meandering.

"Got it," I said triumphantly as I pulled the shoebox from the darkness. The box did indeed contain a deck of cards, some dice, and also some miscellaneous game pieces including chess, checkers, and a Monopoly top hat. There were no game boards.

"Perfect," Pistache commented. "Let's see the cards. Everyone gather around up here."

Trudel joined the rest of us at the bar, and Pistache began wildly handling the cards. As drunk as he appeared, he was amazingly adept with the shuffle.

"Didn't you say you did a little magic?" Janie asked him.

"I did, but card tricks aren't really my thing. That is, unless you have another card hiding behind your ear," he said as he winked and playfully pinched her cheek. I have a pretty high tolerance for people hitting on my wife, but this was starting to be a bit much. Janie wasn't exactly pleased either.

"Back off, man," I finally snapped. I could feel myself starting to really dislike this guy. "Really, that's enough."

"Sorry, my friend. I get carried away," he apologized. "Okay, here's the game. There are five of us here, so we deal out 9 cards each, jokers included."

"What about the leftovers?" I asked.

"There will be a nine card blind," he answered with a shrug.

"What's this game called?" Trudel asked.

"I don't know. Uh … Pistache!" Jacques exclaimed.

Trudel already looked like she disapproved.

"This is not a real game?" I asked.

"Of course it's real! Here's what happens: we will begin with clubs. Whoever has the two of clubs lays it down and has to take a drink. We each take turns adding to the pile in a sequence. Three, four, five, etc. We go all the way up to the ace. Whoever has the ace assigns a sip to someone else. That person will then drink and call the next suit."

"Uh, okay," I stammered. Janie gave me a look of slight confusion, and I'm sure she read the same on my face. Fleuse and Trudel looked equally perplexed.

"Think you got it?" Pistache asked.

"I guess," Janie said.

"So only four people drink through the whole deck? The ones who start each suit?" I asked. Feeling drunk, I needed as much explanation as possible.

"Definitely not. You'll see. I have an idea for it. Let's walk through a round. Who has the two of clubs?"

We looked at each other. Fleuse glanced at his hand. "Me," he said as he produced the card and laid it on the bar.

"Excellent," Pistache went on. "Bottoms up."

"Easy," Fleuse said bravely as he took a sip.

"Perfect!" exclaimed Jacques. "Now, who has the three of clubs?"

"I do." Janie said.

"Lay it down, please. See, we are creating a suited run: two through ace of clubs. Fleuse began the run, so he had to drink. Who's next? Four of clubs?"

We all produced the sequence one after another until the ten of clubs could not be produced.

"What happens now?" I asked.

"Well, the ten must be in the blind," Pistache explained. "The streak is broken because no one has it. Who has the jack?"

"I do," Trudel said.

"Great, lay it down and take a drink."

"Why do I have to drink? It's not the start of a suit."

"But you are the first in a new run. Those are the rules," Pistache said.

"You are making them up as you go! Those are not the rules," the opera singer protested.

"No, my dear. I think those are the rules," Fleuse jumped in.

"I am not 'your dear'!" Trudel snapped and took a drink. I wasn't sure if it was a drink because of the game or a drink because she was coping with Fleuse's advances.

"Excellent, thank you Trudel," Pistache said. "Well done." He threw down the queen, the king followed.

"Here's the ace," I said as I lay the final club on the bar.

"That's when you yell, 'Pistache'!" Jacques said.

I laughed. "Pistache!"

"And now you assign a drink to someone."

"Well, I pick you."

"Okay, very well." Pistache took a drink. "Now, since I was picked by the person with the ace, then I call the next suit. I'll say spades. Who has the two of spades?"

"Right here," Janie said. She laid it down.

"One question," I interrupted. "I have a joker. What do I do with that?"

"If you are lucky enough to hold a joker, then it may be used to deflect a drink on to someone else. It's not unlike the ace in that regard."

"Oh, okay. When do I play it?"

"Any time you want."

"So I can just throw it down right now and make you take another drink?"

"I'm sorry, I should have clarified," Pistache went on. "The joker deflects a drink in the sense that it protects you from a drink you don't want. If someone asks you to drink, you can put down the joker and give that drink to someone else."

"I get it now," I said with a nod.

The game had progressed silently as Pistache and I spoke.

"Who has the nine of spades?" Trudel asked.

I threw it down. The ten followed. The game stopped.

"And the jack?" Trudel asked.

Another second of silence.

"The jack is in the blind!" Pistache exclaimed. "Whoever has the queen, produce it and drink!"

Before anyone could move, the curtain again parted and a new face entered the bar. I half expected him to know everyone in the room since that seemed to be the pattern, but the good-looking, plain man smiled slightly when I looked up and he approached the bar.

"Good evening, sir," I said like a real bartender.

"Good evening. A beer, please."

"Sounds good," I replied. The rest looked at him.

"Looks like you are all in the middle of a card game," he noticed.

"Yes," Pistache answered. "In fact, I was just explaining the rules to my friends here. Would you like to join? It could be easily arranged."

"No thank you," the stranger said politely. "I brought a book, so I'll be comfortable somewhere over there. Thanks," he said as I slid him a beer, and he retreated quietly to the tables.

I looked to Janie and whispered, "Who brings a book to a bar at night?"

"I have, actually," she whispered. "He must like it quiet."

"Maybe in the afternoon, sure," I said, "but I've never heard of anyone going out at night with a book to a bar."

"It's not too bad a thing," Janie said.

"So we continue!" Pistache exclaimed. "Where's the king of spades?"

Janie took another sip from her Esprit de la Nuit and threw a card on the bar.

*   *   *

After a few rounds, I began to realize exactly how frequently I was taking sips during Pistache's game. Shouts of "Ace! Drink! Pistache! Hearts! Joker!" were becoming more frequent as we increased our speed of gameplay.

The fourth patron to enter proved even more quiet than Fleuse. He was a detached player in our scene, but I caught him curiously gazing over the pages of his book more than once.

The street performer was beginning to move more and more clumsily. He celebrated every "Pistache!" with a little dance and bow, usually nearly throwing himself to the ground.

Everyone else was really coming around on the game. Even Trudel was smiling more often. There was an instance when she wasn't paying enough attention for Pistache's liking, and he reached over and pulled a card from her hand for her. From what I knew of Trudel, normally this presumptive act and invasion of space would have sent her through the ceiling, but here she easily replied, "Isn't it wonderful how a little nonsense brings people together?"

"Here's the ace! Pistache!" Pistache exclaimed once again. "Oh Fleusie, dear!"

Fleuse looked slowly in his direction. "Yes?"

"Have a drink, and call the next suit."

"This is quite a game, Jacques," Fleuse muttered without lifting his glass.

"Are you running out of steam, my dear man?" Pistache asked.

Fleuse didn't answer.

"Oh no," Pistache continued. "Don't give up now. You just need a little pick-me-up."

He leapt in his direction and grabbed Fleuse's hands. Extending Fleuse's arm, Pistache began swaying him back and forth, humming a soft but lively song. He was trying to dance him back to the game.

"You two are strange," Trudel said.

Janie was smiling.

"C'mon, Jacques. Stop it," Fleuse slurred.

"Someone has to bring you back, Fleusie! Why not me?"

Fleuse shot a look of embarrassment in Trudel's direction.

"You move well, my man," Pistache continued with a playful tone.

Fleuse finally shook himself loose and gently pushed Pistache away. I noticed the stranger with the book watching in quiet amusement.

"I don't need the pick-me-up. I'm fine," Fleuse said while still looking in Trudel's direction. "I call diamonds."

"I have the two," Trudel said.

"Did you like my dancing?" Fleuse whispered to her.

"You were hating it yourself in the moment," she answered. "Now you are proud of it?"

"Of course he's proud," Pistache interjected. "We were good together just now."

Fleuse shot him a disdainful look.

"Who has the three?" I asked. No one answered.

"How about the four?" Pistache added.

Again, no one moved. We all looked at each other.

"What happens if consecutive cards are in the blind?" I asked.

"Then everyone takes a drink! Pistache!" Pistache yelled.

"You're making that up," Trudel accused.

"Yes, I am," he finally admitted. "Are you not having fun?"

"Yes, actually, I am."

"I knew it, Madame von Hugelstein," Pistache said with a smirk.

"But," she added. "That doesn't mean I find you at all funny!"

Pistache brightened. He leaned toward her and threw his arm around her shoulder.

"Madame von Hugelstein, I must tell you! I have met my match!" He laughed heartily and Trudel leaned away. His breath must have had a proof all its own.

"Okay, that's enough of that," she said, grimacing. "You can get off me now." She shrank from under his arm.

"Sorry," Pistache said with a smile more at Fleuse than Trudel as he took a sip of his drink. "Didn't mean to move in on your girl."

"I'm not his girl," Trudel reiterated.

"She's not," Fleuse sighed.

"Let's have a break from the game," I announced. "I feel like we are all going to be hurting tomorrow morning if we keep this pace up."

"Yes, I'm good with that," Janie reinforced.

Fleuse pushed the pile of cards in front of him back toward the group. I could tell he was in agreement.

"It was just getting fun!" Pistache exclaimed.

*   *   *

Janie was alone at a table, scribbling on a napkin. She tends to log ideas the moment she gets them. It's the curse of the artistic. Plus, I knew she needed to clear her head a little. The booze had twisted up everyone's mind. Pistache is a dangerous game.

Fleuse and Jacques were also back out at a table. I couldn't hear them talking, but the conversation looked congenial enough. The stranger had not moved from his post with his book, so that left me alone at the bar with Trudel.

"Is tonight turning out as you expected?" I asked.

She thought for a moment. The liquor had opened her up a little bit. "Not exactly, but it's going alright I suppose."

"That's good to hear. So," I switched gears, "you and Fleuse, huh?"

"No! Of course not!" she exclaimed.

"No, I know. You are clearly still in love with Victor. But, I meant that you used to date or something?"

"It was a long time ago, and it didn't mean anything."

"It seems to mean a little to him now."

"Perhaps it does," she said with a short glance at him over her shoulder.

"I guess it's harmless," I said.

"But annoying," she answered.

"What did you think of my piano playing?"

"Fine," she replied, again without expression. "You should stick to writing the news."

"Well, I wouldn't call it news. I'm usually assigned the most boring stuff. Actually, tonight has made me want to go and be a bartender again. I'm having a really good time."

"Like I said, you should stick to writing the news."

Taking advantage of the break in the action, the stranger among us approached the bar.

"I see that this might be a good time to get another drink," he said, smiling.

"Why's that?" Trudel asked, barely looking up.

"That game seems to have died down a bit, and the bartender doesn't seem too busy," he replied.

"Absolutely, sir. What'll it be?" I answered.

"Another of the same, please."

Following the lead of the stranger, Janie and Pistache were slowly moving back in the direction of the bar. Fleuse remained at the table, lost in his glass.

"You know," I said to the stranger. "We very well may begin another round of the game here. Would you like us to deal you in this time?"

He smiled. "No, it looks full to me."

"Are you sure? It's a made-up game. I'm sure we could find a way to include you," I said with a nod in Pistache's direction.

"Don't look at me," the street performer said with a smile. "The game came through me! I was merely a conduit of the drinking-card-game fates!"

"No, thank you anyway," the stranger said pleasantly. "I was having a fine time just observing."

I went to work on the man's second drink. Alcohol was slowing the bartending. Funny.

"So!" Pistache began as he threw his arms into the air. "Tell us, my friend. What brings you in tonight?"

The stranger looked to Pistache. "Well, I wanted a drink. I happened to see this place as I was walking by. It looked as good a spot as any."

"Well, you couldn't have chosen better, my friend. What are you reading?"

"It is a book of poetry. I found it at a book fair recently."

"Very cool," Janie commented. Both men ignored her.

"Oh yes? Who wrote it?" Pistache asked.

"It's a compilation. Various authors," the stranger said with a shrug.

"I've never heard of him," Pistache said with a laugh, looking to the rest of us for a response.

"I liked the picture on the cover. Poems are short. They are easy to read," the man went on without acknowledging the joke.

"I have actually always thought the opposite," Pistache said. "They are kind of cryptic."

"That's the beauty of them," the stranger answered. "I like to search for the subtle hints at meaning."

"That always just frustrated me," Pistache said.

"Not me. It's what I do. It's like a code to decipher or a treasure to uncover. I like the hunt almost as much as I like the eventual feeling of discovery and release."

"Aren't you a deep one?!" Pistache roared with amusement. "Have you read one yet that you don't understand?"

"No. Eventually, I always figure them out."

The stranger only smiled and nodded as I passed him the drink. There was a quick moment of silence as Pistache looked at the man.

"Well, this exchange has gone on long enough without us knowing each other! Jacques Pistache!" Pistache exclaimed as he thrust his hand into the stranger's grasp. "It's a treat to meet you, finally!"

"Julian Renard, and it certainly is."

"With you watching from the corner, it felt as though you were our audience, and we the players. I'm glad you are a part of the show now, Monsieur Renard!"

"I have been waiting for the right time, to be truthful."

"Oh, I figured you were content to watch."

The two shook hands for a few moments in silence. I almost had to smile at how awkward the exchange had become so quickly. Now that they had introduced themselves, there didn't seem to be anything more for either to say.

Finally, Julian continued. "So, Monsieur Pistache ..."

"Yes?" the street performer answered slowly.

"How long do you think it will be before Madame von Hugelstein realizes that her ring is missing?"

Trudel immediately shot a look toward her hand. "My ring!" She gasped.

Pistache frowned at Renard.

"Jacques, mon ami. Don't you think this charade has run its course?" the stranger said softly.

Chapter VII.

The golden ballroom at Peukington Manor glowed with grandeur. Spinning couples turned to the soaring strings of a small orchestra, and many more guests stood among a sea of round dinner tables, laughing and conversing. The air was full of floral breezes and champagne fizzes.

Jacques Pistache swam slowly between tables, waiting to strike. Dressed in his black-tie best, no one could have suspected that the man didn't know a soul at the fête. He sipped from his drink as he walked and smiled pleasantly at anyone who caught his eye.

The street performer had already been at the party for about an hour. He'd spoken with several other guests. Everyone seemed gracious, but he was slightly disappointed. He had yet to see the man he'd come to meet. Surely, Lavaar Peukington should have arrived by then. Why would he be late to his own daughter's engagement party?

Peukington was one of the richest residents of Paris. A successful businessman, he'd gained fame through large real estate dealings. His company financed scientific research grants, owned thousands of patents on products in all industries, and published a fashion magazine. Still, Lavaar Peukington was almost never seen in public.

Pistache was different. He attended gatherings of all kinds. He often met many people, without conversing for more than a few minutes with anyone in particular. All of this superficial glad-handing was part of his trained behavior. His livelihood depended upon every handshake and people's willingness to be physically moved. With every pat on the back or brush of the arm, Pistache steered the momentum of his subject. He lived in the personal space of others.

Jacques Pistache was a pickpocket.

Considering himself to be part magician and part dancer, Pistache mastered the fundamentals of his craft. However, other challenges often kept him from succeeding. Self-awareness was not one of his strong suits, nor was staying sober enough to properly perform.

Still, history proved that he was good at it. The pickpocket imagined the expression of the mayor's wife when she realized her diamond earring was gone—a crowning moment in his career. He loved the deception almost as much as the money.

His sense of humor was evident in his work. He could steal belts or shirt buttons. Pennies tucked in loafers were often targets. The pickpocket enjoyed giving the coins back to their original owners for luck. Victims rarely realized that the pennies were actually theirs.

Pistache had been anticipating the party at Peukington Manor for weeks. He traveled to this posh neighborhood in Paris for one simple reason: to take something from Lavaar Peukington himself. Given the man's fortune, surely he must be a walking goldmine.

The pickpocket had received a fresh martini when another partygoer sauntered up to the bar.

"Evening," the stranger said.

"Good evening," Pistache replied.

"What a night, no?"

"That's right," the pickpocket smiled. "A fantastic party."

"Yes," the man replied as he stuffed a euro into the tip jar. "He sure knows how to be a host!"

"He does," Pistache agreed, casually brushing the man's tuxedo pocket with the back of his hand. Nothing.

"Did you have trouble with the valet?" the man said. "I thought the young man was difficult."

"Well, I didn't think he was bad," Pistache lied. The pickpocket had hired a taxi to make the drive. Few people arrived at this party so unceremoniously.

"Just think twice before you tip him," the man said as he lifted his two drinks from the bar.

"Oh, I will."

"You just never know if those guys are working for you, or against you."

Pistache nodded as he sipped his drink. "Have you been to one of Monsieur Peukington's parties before?"

The stranger nodded as he took the first sips of his drink.

"When can we expect the host?" Pistache asked, lightly touching the edges of woman's dress behind him.

"He'll be down any minute. Did you see the seafood spread?"

"I did."

"Well enjoy yourself. The dance floor calls," the man said, raising his drink as he left.

"Nice meeting you," Pistache answered.

"Nice meeting you," the man said, slipping away into the crowd.

In that exact moment, Lavaar Peukington entered with much pomp. From where he stood at the bar, Pistache did not have a direct line of sight. In fact, his back was turned to the scene. Still, the pickpocket could see everything happening through the large mirror behind the rows of bottles of booze.

Peukington walked like a wealthy man, hard jawline lifted and shoulders relaxed. Jacques could see the perfectly pressed breast of his tuxedo, the flash of a bright white scarf, and the glint of gold cufflinks. The pickpocket would love to have a closer look at those.

As one entire section of the room seemed to gravitate toward the gentleman, Pistache remained stoic with his back to the action. His instincts yearned to go straight to Peukington, but he knew better. He waited at the bar to watch the man move, casually exchanging a few words with the bartenders.

Finally seeing his moment of opportunity, the pickpocket entered the crowd, leaving his drink behind. He slipped between shoulders, involuntarily noticing prizes buried under thin fabrics on either side. A watch passed on his right, a wallet on his left. The pickpocket resisted the urge, hoping for a larger payout.

Did Peukington's cufflinks have diamonds? Would there be a key to a safe in his pocket? Did he wear an heirloom watch? As questions swirled in his head, he saw the host truly for the first time as the crowd briefly parted.

Tall and slender, Lavaar Peukington was in top shape. He sported a neatly trimmed mustache and a full head of hair. Bright eyes were framed by crow's feet, surely earned on the beaches of southern France. The man was charmingly happy and greeting people as if he were running for public office.

"What a rich asshole," Jacques muttered to himself.

The crowds thickened as Jacques approached Peukington. Everyone surrounding the man was waiting to speak with him. Pistache even noticed the stranger from the bar hovering close by, eyeing the crowd, looking for his own opportunity.

The pickpocket watched Peukington closely. The wealthy host was deliberate, confident, and slightly protective. A waiter passed, and Jacques accepted a glass of wine.

Close enough to hear the rich man's voice over the roar of the room, Peukington pronounced every letter in every word. Jacques was rarely intimidated, but his target appeared formidable. The pickpocket felt already out matched, patiently worming close enough to offer a handshake.

"Monsieur Peukington!" He thrust his hand forward and smiled brightly. "I am Claude Pennington. We met a few years back at the Parisian Society benefit," he lied.

"I remember the event, but I must apologize. I meet so many good people." Peukington replied, without reintroducing himself.

Pistache had hoped to sense some weakness in the man's handshake. He didn't.

"I wouldn't expect you to remember. My company catered the event," Pistache continued.

"I had a nice time that night, and I'm glad that you could join us this evening," Peukington said, eager to greet the next guest. "Please enjoy the wine. Tonight's a good one for celebrating."

And with that, he moved on.

Pistache barely had enough time to introduce himself, let alone properly assess the man. Additionally, Peukington's lack of sincerity bothered the pickpocket. He detested the man's air.

Plus, there was that iron handshake. Usually a test of his prey's willingness to be controlled, this greeting was statuesque and uncompromising. Lavaar Peukington moved for no one. Jacques would not be able to operate the man easily.

To get anything off of him, the pickpocket would have to be extra careful. Pistache welcomed the challenge, but he needed time to reevaluate. He retreated, gulping the wine and rethought his plan at a table.

*   *   *

An hour ticked off the clock slowly, and Pistache didn't feel any better about his chances with the host. He began distracting himself by recounting items he'd already nabbed: a lapel pin, a gold band, and a tie clip. Jacques had only targeted things easily lost by their owners and unlikely to arouse suspicion. After lifting a diamond-encrusted pocket watch or necklace, he would have to disappear quickly before anyone noticed it was missing.

Peukington had gotten a good look at the pickpocket's face. Pistache assumed that his target was not the kind of man to forget many people. This may have already raised Peukington's suspicions, since they had presumably met once before. Jacques wondered if he understood the man enough to proceed. On the other hand, was he reading too much into his prey?

Always maintaining a general awareness of Peukington's whereabouts in the room, these thoughts kept Pistache busy. He knew his actions would need to be well timed and the moment chosen carefully. But to his surprise, it wouldn't be up to him.

Suddenly, Jacques heard Peukington's voice speaking directly behind him. His ears twitched as the host greeted guests, and he wondered how Peukington had gotten so close to him. Was the wealthy man in the pickpocket's trap, or was it the other way around?

Jacques stood immediately. He decided that it was time to make his move, whether or not he felt ready. There wasn't a second left to think any further.

He had act quickly, so Pistache purposefully tripped a random partygoer near Peukington. Falling over himself, the unsuspecting man fell directly into the host. Pistache lunged for Peukington's wrist.

In a moment just long enough to blink, Pistache flicked his fingers and unclasped Peukington's left cufflink.

"Oops," the pickpocket muttered, as if genuinely surprised by the falling man. "Excuse me, monsieur!"

Pistache felt the cufflink slip from his grasp. It hadn't even hit the ground yet, but Jacques knew he had dropped it just as he removed it from the shirt. It would be too obvious to grab it from the floor or even acknowledge it.

Slightly panicked, Pistache launched into an effort to save the moment. Thrusting himself into Peukington, Jacques reached for the host's breast coat pocket. He hoped for anything and blindly pinched an object inside.

"Yes, excuse me!" Peukington blurted, pushing Pistache away. Turning his attention to the fallen man, he said, "Are you okay?"

"I think so," the partygoer stammered.

Pistache noticed the stranger from the bar dart from the crowd to help the fallen man get up. Peukington adjusted his tux coat.

"He had better not have another drink, wouldn't you say?" Pistache said to Peukington, nervously laughing.

"I'd say so," he answered, annoyed.

It was a clean lift.

"Is this your cufflink, Monsieur Peukington?" the partygoer asked as he stood. He'd picked up the item.

"It is. Thank you," the host said, eyeing the piece.

Pistache was already halfway to the exit.

*   *   *

As he hurried down the sidewalk, the warm evening air brought a welcome sense of space back to Pistache. He couldn't help but sneak a smile as he felt the object in his pocket. He was able to shoot a quick glance behind him. No one followed him.

After walking carefully in shadow, he reached a cab in front of a modestly lit café. After exchanging a few pleasantries with the driver, they were off for the heart of Paris, and Pistache turned his attention to his loot in the dark backseat of the car. He removed the small metal object from his jacket pocket and stared at it for a moment.

"Just a coin?" he muttered to himself.

"I'm sorry?" the driver asked from the front seat.

"Nothing, sorry," Pistache clarified, waving him off. Soft flashes of light moved over it as the taxi passed streetlamp after streetlamp. The soft yellow strobe only made it harder for the inebriated pickpocket to examine the object.

It carried considerable weight for a coin its size. It was larger than most coins he'd seen. A man's face adorned one scarred side, defiant yet calm. Pistache guessed he wouldn't recognize him, even without the abrasion.

Without a substantial lift, the pickpocket was disappointed with the night. He'd spend the rest of the evening hovering quietly over drinks in a café, the stolen currency resting on the table in front of him. Barmaids greeted him warmly, but he just nodded. He remained uncharacteristically silent, exchanging looks with the man on the coin.

Chapter VIII.

"A pickpocket?!" Trudel yelled.

"Fill them in, Monsieur Pistache," Renard said calmly.

The two men remained locked in a stare. The tenor between all the players had shifted in the room. An atmosphere of distrust suddenly hung in the air.

"I may not have been entirely honest with you all," Pistache said, finally breaking eye contact with Renard.

No one moved.

"Let me guess," Renard said to Janie and me. "He told you that he's a street performer."

"I am a street performer!" Pistache protested.

"Well, true. But, not because you are passionate about your craft as a singer or dancer or whatever."

"I knew it," Trudel softly hummed.

Renard continued, "Did he do some of his awful voices for you? Or maybe he tried to teach you his version of tap dancing?"

Pistache remained silent.

"Explain it for them, Jacques," the stranger said.

Pistache did not say anything.

"Well, I'll take it upon myself to introduce you properly to the room." He turned to the rest of us and continued. "It's all fake. It's all meant to distract."

Fleuse blinked. "Do you two know each other?"

"In fact, we do," Renard answered, turning. "We've known each other for some time, actually. Well, maybe that's going a little too far. We have met, and I definitely feel as though I know him. I can't say how he feels about me, though." He turned again toward

Pistache. "Actually, I don't think he remembers our first meeting."

"Of course I do," Pistache finally broke his silence. Despite lifting his glass to swig for some apparent courage, he was sounding remarkably more sober than he had been even moments earlier. "Peukington's party."

"Oh! Very good, Jacques," Renard said. "I wasn't sure that you recognized me."

"How could I miss you, the unassuming partygoer who had an issue with the valet? Was that some kind of act?"

Renard smiled and shook his head. "No. That guy was really terrible. When I got back into my car, the seat was all ..." He struggled for the correct word. "... adjusted."

"I figured it was your way of disarming strangers at your boss's party."

"You were over-analyzing me. I was actually off duty when we spoke."

"Well, don't think that I didn't notice the way you rushed to Peukington's side the moment he entered," Pistache said. "Or, how you happened to be right there to help that guy off the floor. I don't think you took your eyes off Peukington from the moment he entered the room. In the moment, I thought you might have been his lover!"

Renard laughed heartily. "I see. Well, that's fine."

"Are you his bodyguard?" Fleuse interjected, shyly.

"You don't see me guarding him right now, do you?" Renard answered without looking in his direction.

Pistache took a beat. I could see him choosing his words carefully, as if deciding upon a move in a chess match. "When you came in here tonight, it took me a few minutes to place you. But, the way you kept your eyes on us, I began to feel your arrival was not an accident."

"You're a perceptive person, Jacques," Renard continued. "I'll at least give you that. But your drunken act only masks the real facts. First off, you really do drink too much for someone who needs to rely so heavily on motor skills."

Pistache took a drink as if he were challenging Renard's claims.

Renard continued. "Let me guess. A decade ago, you could rattle off everything in each of your pockets at any moment?"

Pistache swallowed hard and didn't acknowledge the challenge.

"But nowadays," Renard continued, "I'm guessing you have to pat yourself down as a reminder of where you put everything.

Pistache began to grit his teeth. Janie shot me another glance. She had been right. This was better drama than anything we could have seen in a theater.

"Go on," Renard persisted. "Let's see it. No one is going to do anything about it. You're not in trouble here. You are among friends. Plus, you like games, so this will be fun."

Pistache stood motionless.

"C'mon, Jacques. Play along. So, let's hear it. What's in your pockets?" Renard repeated.

"Start by giving my ring back," Trudel snapped.

Pistache began to reach for a pocket.

"Remember, Jacques," Renard said with a cautionary yet playful tone. "Announce everything that you are going to present before you present it. That's the game. Can you really remember where you've put everything, or have you gotten too sloppy?"

For a moment, I thought Pistache would storm out. I then realized that Renard had cleverly, albeit casually, positioned himself between the curtain and

Pistache. Given the pickpocket's skeletal physique, it would have been foolish of him to challenge the more substantive Renard.

Fleuse and Trudel watched, seemingly holding their breath. I noticed each of them finally sneak a drink of their cocktails.

"Since we are just playing games here and having a little fun," Pistache began slowly without unlocking his stare from Renard. "We'll start with my front jacket pocket and Trudel's ring."

Trudel leaned forward in time to see Pistache produce her ring from his jacket and place it on the bar. She leapt up and seized it. As she repositioned it on her finger, she glared at Pistache and retreated to her table.

"One for one," Renard smiled.

"In my left hip pocket, you will all find an ace." He pulled out the ace of spades. Hoping for humor, he softly exclaimed "Pistache!" as he threw it down on the bar. No one laughed.

"Well done," Renard said.

"I didn't take much from all of you tonight," Pistache went on. "Truly, I was going to probably give it all back," he said as he reached in his pocket and dropped Janie's necklace and my watch on to the table.

"How did you do that?" I asked. I hadn't even noticed that my watch had walked off. I immediately took inventory and realized that something else was also missing. "And my wallet!"

"Take it easy. Here," Pistache said casually as he laid it on the bar for me.

"But, how did you ...?"

"A magician never shares his secrets."

"You're not a magician," Renard snapped. "It's all his distraction act. While he does terrible impersonations ..."

"Impressions," Pistache corrected.

"Whatever. While he does terrible impressions, he wraps his arm around you, or makes up stupid games to engage you, then robs you."

Janie was busy fastening her necklace. She gave me a look. For the first time this evening, she was obviously not having fun. I considered grabbing her and running for the door.

"Notice that he's also left the game," Renard continued, breaking Janie's and my silent sidebar.

"I've been right about everything so far!" Pistache protested.

"Not exactly," Renard answered. "You did not identify the last three items. It's a trick that you masked with conversation just now."

"I knew they were there."

"Sure you did. Anything else?"

"I have Fleuse's watch too."

Surprised at hearing his name, Fleuse checked his wrist and immediately raised his head. He didn't say anything, but the look of betrayal was boundless. He rose and approached Pistache.

"Here you go, my friend," Pistache said. "I was going to give it all back tonight. I was just playing around."

"Okay," Fleuse mustered, examining his watch.

"There should be more," Renard urged.

"I do have another ace." He reached into the inside of his coat pocket. He pulled out not one but two cards from our game of Pistache. Only this time, neither were aces. He threw them onto the bar.

"See what I'm talking about?" Renard asked the room.

Pistache looked confused. He seemed to be silently retracing his steps.

"After a certain point, you can't keep track of what you take," Renard said with a smile. "I bet you didn't even know that you accidentally nabbed two cards."

"A simple mistake," Pistache said. "If that is the only one I made, then I'd say I'm still doing alright."

"If that's what you think," Renard answered.

"Did you see me do any of it?" Pistache asked him.

"No, you still move pretty quickly for a drunk guy. But, I could see the opportunities. I knew when most of them happened. I just couldn't catch all the details. I've been observing you for a few weeks. At first I could barely keep up, but I'm familiar with your methods by now."

"Who are you again?" Fleuse finally spoke up.

"As I said, Julian Renard," he said as he made his way to Fleuse. "And you are Fleuse Newman, the excellent clockmaker. It is nice to finally meet you face-to-face."

"You are familiar with my work?" Fleuse skeptically answered as they shook hands. "Do you know one of my customers?"

"Fleuse," Pistache interrupted. "Are you missing this? He has been following us. Watching us. You as well."

Fleuse looked horrified.

"I'm afraid he's right, Monsieur Newman," Renard confirmed. "I work for a very wealthy businessman. His name is Lavaar Peukington. Do you know him?"

"Obviously," Pistache muttered under his breath.

"Well, maybe not so obvious," Renard said. "I don't know how close the two of you are. I can't be sure what you've told Fleuse here about your profession. After all, you did just take his watch."

"I know who Monsieur Peukington is," Fleuse answered softly with a nod.

Janie and I watched in silence, frozen by the drama unfolding in the room.

"You know that he knows who Monsieur Peukington is," Pistache said to Renard. "Otherwise, you wouldn't have been following him."

"Good point," Renard said.

"So you're … what?" Pistache asked. "His right-hand man?"

"Well, I've worked for him for some time now," Renard went on. "I'd say that I'm best described as his renaissance man. I do many different tasks."

"Why have you been following Fleuse and Jacques?" Trudel finally spoke.

"Well, I wouldn't say that I've been following them exclusively."

"You follow other people, too?" she asked, suddenly suspicious.

"Well not many, but some. I have been keeping an eye on you as well," Renard said to her.

"That's outrageous!" she sung. "Why?!"

"It's not that outrageous," Pistache added with an eye roll. "Can't you see what he's getting at?"

"My particular assignment is to locate something very valuable for Monsieur Peukington," Renard went on.

"The coin!" I heard Fleuse whisper in defeat.

Again Pistache rolled his eyes. "Of course the coin, Fleuse."

"What coin?" Janie blurted out. I was curious as well.

"Well, I believe Monsieur Pistache here took a coin from Monsieur Peukington a few weeks ago."

Pistache finally slumped into a chair. He already knew the story.

"It is a valuable coin," Renard continued, "very old. You see, it has been in Monsieur Peukington's family for many generations. It began as a souvenir of an important era in French history. It dates back to the reign of kings. It's seen revolution and violence, tyranny, the rise and fall of an empire, and so on. It has been in the possession of Monsieur Peukington's ancestors the entire time. Therefore, it's an heirloom, and he believes that it brings him bon chance."

"It's his lucky penny," I muttered.

"Honey, let's go," Janie said as she broke my gaze.

She was right. I wasn't feeling great about being involved with this. Our fun night in the bar had taken a very bizarre turn. I knew that it would be the stuff of a great story later, but in the moment I was becoming increasingly nervous.

"Well, thank you all for an incredibly entertaining evening. We'll leave you to it," I said, reaching for Janie as we stepped out from behind the bar.

"Well, hold on for one moment please, my American friend," Renard said. His tone was unthreatening, but he slowly stepped closer to the curtain, blocking our exit. "The thing is, you can't leave just yet."

"Why not?" I asked, fearing something terrible was about to happen.

"Well, I just need the coin before anyone goes anywhere."

"Well, I don't have it!" I said.

"I know," Renard calmly answered. "But then again, I don't know."

"What?" I asked. "How could I have it? I don't even know what it looks like!"

"We're on vacation!" Janie added. "We just got here two days ago!"

"Calm down, please. See, I have kept my eyes on everyone for the last few weeks, and I am sure that none of them have the coin. This bar has remained dark and under lock and key for that entire time."

Then it hit me. "Oh my God."

"What, honey?" Janie asked.

"I saw you," I said to Renard. "This morning."

Renard looked doubtful.

"I know I did," I continued. "You were in different clothes, but I saw you on the street, outside the hotel."

Finally understanding, he nodded. "You may have."

"No, you looked right at me from the archway on the sidewalk."

"Like I said, I've been watching the hotel and the Bon Parisien."

"And then I saw you again," I continued. "You ran in here a little while later. I barely saw you, but I know I did."

"I've been able to sneak in here once or twice," he confirmed. "I haven't found the coin, though. But, when I saw the lights come on tonight and attract all these parasites," he said motioning at the others, "I realized they believe the same thing I do."

Everyone exchanged looks with one another. No one moved.

"And what's that?" I asked.

Renard stated simply, "the coin is somewhere in this bar."

Chapter IX.

Afternoon sun brightened the Bon Parisien, erasing shadows. A scratchy record played, gently popping away over twenties-era band music. Victor Laquer wiped down the bar in large slow circles, breathing to the rhythm of each pass.

He had been the bartender at the Hôtel des Bretons all summer, often alone on his shifts. The place wasn't exactly buzzing with activity, and he was worried. His bills were piling up, and Victor was starting to sweat. He didn't think he could keep his apartment beyond the next month or two. Being an accountant had been more lucrative.

The bartender tried to forget about his troubles for the moment. He focused on the dark wood as he held his rag. At one time, perhaps he could have seen his reflection growing more and more visible in the varnish as he cleaned. But now, enough guests had come and gone to take the shine with them.

He looked up when the doors suddenly opened. For a brief moment, the sounds of traffic and the buzz of Paris drowned out the soft music. The neighborhood was generally low-key, but it was still the city. Two men entered, immediately shifting the tone of the room.

"Fleuse Newman," Victor said as he identified a familiar face.

"Bonjour, Victor," Fleuse answered kindly.

Victor noticed the short, thin man accompanying Fleuse. The man's brown sport coat looked almost too small. It didn't match his pants. His dark brown hair clung to his forehead. He seemed exhausted, and Victor thought the man might have actually been in a brawl earlier that day. There weren't any bruises or signs of a fight, but his walk was weary.

"This is a friend of mine," Fleuse continued. "Victor Laquer, Jacques Pistache."

"Bonjour," Pistache said.

"Bonjour, Monsieur Pistache," Victor answered pleasantly, followed by a close-lipped smile. "What may I get you, gentlemen?"

"Jacques?" Fleuse deferred.

"A whiskey please," Pistache answered.

"Excellent," Victor said with a smile. "Fleuse?"

"A beer, please."

"Very good."

Pistache looked around the room. Despite the cordial greeting, something about the new man made Victor feel a little uneasy. Fleuse and Jacques were an unlikely pair. Victor would not have predicted their friendship. Pistache had the look of someone casing the room. The bartender had trained himself to notice behavior like that.

"I like this place," Pistache observed. "Very comfortable."

"It is," Victor said, eyeing the man.

"Fleuse tells me you're an accountant?" Pistache asked, returning his gaze to the bartender.

"Well, not any more, actually," Victor answered.

"Retired to be become a bartender? Excellent!" Pistache exclaimed.

Victor frowned. "Not exactly." He pushed the drinks toward the men.

Pistache raised his glass to the bartender.

"Are you expecting Trudel in today?" Fleuse asked.

Victor noticed how quickly Fleuse mentioned her name every time he visited.

"She should be," Victor said without looking up. "I think she was planning on dropping in after a matinée."

"What show is she in now?" Fleuse asked.

"I can't remember," Victor lied. He didn't want to perpetuate a conversation about a relationship that made Fleuse jealous. He knew they had a history.

"Is she a performer?" Pistache asked.

"She is a singer," Fleuse answered.

"Oh, wonderful!" Pistache exclaimed. He looked toward Victor. "So am I!"

"You're terrible, though," Fleuse said.

"I am not!"

"Cut it out," Fleuse groaned, fully aware of Pistache's act.

"You are a performer as well?" Victor asked.

"I mostly do impersonations," Pistache said.

"So do you have a closet full of Elvis Presley jumpsuits or something?" Victor grunted.

"No, I mostly just do the voices."

"So you do impressions?" the bartender asked.

"Yes! That's right. Is that different than impersonations?" Pistache responded.

"Impersonators dress the part," Victor clarified. "Impressionists do voices."

"I'll keep that in mind next time I tell someone what I do," Pistache asked. "How do you know so much about all this?"

"I can't get Trudel to be quiet about how much she hates mimes, jugglers, and impersonators."

"Then it's a good thing that I do impressions," Pistache joked.

"I'm sure she hates that, too," Victor said.

"Just don't let him start dancing in here," Fleuse said dryly.

"How do you two know each other?" Victor asked.

"We met years ago," Fleuse explained. "We are mainly in touch now about business."

"The clocks?" The bartender asked.

"Yes, of course."

"The best way to understand it is that I supply some of the raw materials," Pistache added.

"Oh I see," Victor said. "A supplier. Well, I help Fleuse with his books. I am familiar with his business. Are you a mechanics guy? Woods? Hands and faces guy?"

"I've always thought of myself as a legs guy," Pistache said, laughing.

The other two men snickered, and there was a brief pause in the conversation.

"That's funny," Victor finally said. "But really, I love his clocks. What do you do?"

Pistache took another drink, carefully considering an answer. "Actually," he said, "I deal with mostly gems and some precious metals."

Victor took a quick look over to Fleuse. "I see," he said pleasantly. "You are a jeweler?"

"Yes, kind of," Pistache explained with a sip.

"Interesting," Victor said softly.

"That's actually why we're here today," Fleuse began.

"Oh?" Victor answered.

"Go ahead, Pistache," Fleuse urged.

Pistache reached into his pocket, pulled out a coin, and placed it on the bar in front of Victor.

"Do you know what this is?" the pickpocket asked genuinely.

"It's a coin," Victor deadpanned.

Fleuse snickered.

Seeming annoyed, Pistache looked to the clockmaker before continuing. "Right. It's a coin. I mean do you know how much it's worth?"

Victor reached for his reading glasses behind the bar. Still wary of Pistache, his curiosity about the coin overcame his skepticism of the man. Picking up the object, Victor moved toward a small lamp behind the bar.

"Let me get a good look here," the bartender muttered.

The two men stood quietly drinking on the other side of the bar while Victor examined the coin. He noticed its weight. Time, touches, and the dark insides of pockets had worn down the once artfully distinct engravings on each side. It was barely readable.

"I will have to look it up, but this is likely a mid-eighteenth century coin. I've seen others that have a similar look. Doesn't seem to be the feel of pure gold. Not sure how much it's worth."

"But, it's maybe worth something?" Fleuse asked.

"Maybe," the bartender answered.

"Do you recognize the royal on it?" Fleuse asked.

Victor scrutinized the piece. "Looks like Louis XVI. It's hard to tell, though. There is an abrasion across his face."

"Will that affect the price of the coin in today's terms?" Pistache asked.

"Almost definitely, but it's hard to tell," Victor said as he held it toward the light. "If it were an error during minting, it may make it worth more. But, that scenario seems unlikely to me. It isn't the mark of machinery. It still could be worth something, though."

"Has to be," Pistache added.

Victor looked up. "Why would it have to be?"

"Well," Pistache stammered a bit. "Something that old, wouldn't it have to be worth something?"

"I suppose. Where did you get it?" Victor asked. "Have you had it long?"

Pistache and Fleuse exchanged quick looks. "I picked it up at a flea market. I thought it looked good," Pistache lied.

Victor looked to Fleuse, who diverted his gaze momentarily. Victor placed the coin back on the bar. "Then how much did you pay for it?"

"Not too much," Pistache managed. "I can't really remember the exact price. I picked up a lot of little trinkets that day."

Victor's eyes narrowed, and he took a beat.

"Okay, gentlemen. I'm not an idiot," the bartender said. "There are a few things wrong with your story. First, I have been Fleuse's accountant for several years. Nowhere in his dealings is there mention of working alongside a proper jeweler."

Fleuse and Pistache looked uneasy.

"But, I have seen his finished products and more than once noticed their quality," Victor continued. "I saw things on some clocks that I know I didn't see on the books, but I've always kept my mouth shut. I've stayed out of it on purpose, but this specific instance really doesn't add up."

Fleuse and Pistache stared into their drinks.

"Plus Jacques, you don't look or dress like any jeweler that I've ever seen. At least look like you're trying to play the part," Victor said.

"Well …" Pistache began.

"Wait," Victor interrupted. "Secondly, no one comes across this coin for flea market prices. I don't know how much it's worth, but I know how much it isn't worth—and that's less than say 100 euros at the most misguided estimation. Sometimes, something like this could sell for more than 3,000 euros. So based on what you've said, I think that this coin was acquired dishonestly."

"I can explain," Fleuse began.

"You don't have to," Victor cut him off. "I am a little surprised to find that you've resorted to dealing with a common thief."

"A common thief?!" Pistache took offense.

Victor raised his eyebrows at the man, daring him to prove his innocence.

"Okay," Pistache continued. "Fine. All the cards are on the table. I take things off people. I don't just rob them. I gently lift without anyone noticing."

"A street pickpocket," Victor grunted disdainfully.

"Well, I can do it on the street, yes. But, there isn't any glory in that. I'm a party crasher. I can do it with class."

"A coyote in a tuxedo," Victor muttered.

"Well, I steal objects," Pistache explained. "Usually, they're worth a lot. I could try to sell them as is, but often their owners try to hunt them down. So, I go to Fleuse here. He shapes them, crafts them, or melts them down and puts them in a clock."

"You're unexplained petty cash expenditures," Victor said to Fleuse.

"We're just not sure what to do with this coin," the clockmaker added.

Pistache continued. "Something potentially this valuable might be worth much more if it were not melted down for the precious metal. Its current state might be the very source of its value."

Victor saw an opportunity. Without having earned much in the Bon Parisien and a few weeks away from bankruptcy, the bartender realized that the coin could be his ticket out of financial trouble.

"So," Pistache continued, "I figured that maybe we try to move the coin unaltered. That is, if it's worth it."

"Has the owner come looking for it?" Victor asked, his mind racing.

"Well, not yet."

"But," Fleuse added. "We believe that he might."

"Why's that?" Victor asked.

"Well, it's Lavaar Peukington," Fleuse said.

Victor was taken aback. "Wow. He's famous."

"Yeah," Pistache said, proudly.

"I've heard he's dangerous," Victor said.

"Yep," Pistache answered again with pride.

"How did you get it? I mean, how did you get close to him?" Victor was trying to think it through.

"I attended one of his parties and took it right out of his coat pocket."

"Hmm," Victor thought aloud. "Bold."

"So do you think there would be a way to move this?" Fleuse asked.

"I do," Victor said hesitantly. "Peukington probably doesn't play around, though. He's obviously noticed it's gone by now."

"Definitely," Pistache said, smirking.

"The first step is going to be assessing this coin's value," Victor guessed.

"That's why we came to you," Pistache said, irritated.

"Well, I have collected, yes," Victor said, "but I don't know the details about every coin ever made. I've actually sold off most of my collection. Still, I have a contact who can pinpoint exactly when and where this one was minted. He's helped me in the past. May I take it to him?"

"We were hoping you'd know someone who might have an answer in case you didn't," Fleuse said.

"Can we trust this guy?" Pistache added.

"Oh yes," Victor answered. "As I said, I've used him many times before."

"I would be happy to go with you," Pistache said.

"Are you sure that's what you want, though?" Victor answered. "If Peukington does in fact try to hunt you down, wouldn't you like to not have the coin for a while? It might be helpful for you to throw them off the scent in case he finds you."

"He has a point," Fleuse reassured Pistache. "We can trust Victor."

The bartender continued, "Fleuse, I have a feeling this coin will be worth a good deal of money, especially if it was in Lavaar Peukington's pocket. I would accept a modest fee for the transportation and estimation of value for the coin."

"And you won't mind putting yourself in danger?" Fleuse asked.

"Well, I won't really be in danger," he answered. "No one really expects me to have it. They don't know to look for me."

"Peukington, you mean?" Fleuse asked for clarification.

"Yes," Victor answered. "Plus, it will only be for a short time anyway. Just long enough to get an idea of its worth."

Fleuse and Pistache silently conferred. "That sounds reasonable," Newman said.

"As long as the coin is worth an adequate sum," Pistache added protecting his own interests. "If it's not worth anything, your fee would have to be pretty small."

"I understand," Victor said. "That seems fair."

"Are you sure you are okay doing this?" Fleuse finally asked him.

"I assure you, I'll be fine," Victor answered, seeing a possible solution to his financial troubles.

Chapter X.

"Let me make sure that I'm understanding this correctly," I thought aloud as we stood in the bar, however many drinks in. "You guys have been stalking this bar until it reopened—and in some cases stalking each other—just to find a coin that might be worth a little money?"

"Well, not just a little money," Pistache said.

"Okay, so let's say it's worth two thousand euros," I went on. "That would be an incredible price for an old coin, no? What happens next? A few of you split it? If Julian here finds it, it just heads back to the owner? Why all the fuss for a couple hundred euros?"

As I spoke, I glanced at Janie. I could tell she had the same inquiry.

"I remember when Victor first mentioned it," Trudel stated. "He was excited about it. He wouldn't have been if it had been small change. He was used to dealing with big numbers, investments, and so on."

"She's right. The coin is actually quite a bit more valuable than any of these people predicted," Renard stated calmly.

I looked to the rest of them. Everyone was silent. It became obvious that whatever Renard was about to say was only news to Janie and me.

"On top of the enormous sentimental value of the object for Monsieur Peukington, it's known among collectors as the rarest of its kind."

Pistache jumped in. "Victor knew it. When we saw him next, he could barely contain himself."

"Due to the crudeness and inexactitude of the minting pre-revolution, there were many imperfections on currency," Renard explained. "Coins like this one are not solely made valuable by errors in minting. There has to be more. In this coin's case, it began as a 100-franc coin, so it has Louis XVI's image pressed into it. But, it was Napoleon who made his mark on it."

"Literally," Pistache huffed.

Janie and I looked at each other.

"What do you mean by 'literally'?" Janie asked.

"It is said," Renard continued, "that Napoleon led his troops into battle. A musket ball struck him, and he would have been killed in action if it weren't for this coin in his pocket. It is not possible to know for certain if this tale is true. The coin itself is damaged from the bullet, but it was not likely a direct hit if it occurred."

Pistache added, "The bullet left a mark right across the face of Louis XVI."

Breaking his silence, Fleuse mused, "Symbolism for the revolution."

All were quiet as the story sunk in, but I couldn't help laughing. Janie was in similar shape. Her facial expression said it all.

"Yeah, right," she said softly.

If the others heard her say it, they chose to ignore it. Renard continued. "We all know Napoleon's story, and apparently this coin never left his side after that. Upon his death, the coin passed to his kin. It's been in his family ever since."

"Gold couldn't stop a bullet without just crumpling, right?" Janie asked. "I mean, is it really all that strong of a metal?"

"Victor guessed that there was iron in it as well," Fleuse added.

"And nickel," Pistache said.

"That's correct," Renard said. "But really mostly iron."

"Okay, let's pretend I believe that for a second," Janie said as she searched for understanding. "So this Peukington guy is a descendant of Napoleon?"

"Really?" I asked.

"Well," Janie continued, "they said that the coin never left Napoleon's family."

"That's right," Renard answered. "That makes the coin a relic of a bygone era of kings, the lucky penny of an emperor, and the treasured heirloom of one of today's most influential and powerful businessmen—a direct descendent of the original owner himself."

"So how much did it wind up being worth?" I asked, still mostly disbelieving the story.

"Well, even if the coin didn't have that story, it would be worth more than face value," Renard explained. Fleuse nodded in agreement. Pistache slowly sipped through another drink.

"It was only one of a few 100-franc pieces minted in 1789, before the revolution turned the city upside down," Renard continued. "It was also one of the only pieces minted partially in iron, due to a shortage that year of gold. But above all, it saved the life of an emperor and altered the course of France's history."

"So … it's worth … what?" I asked again.

Pausing for effect, Renard finally stated frankly, "It's worth one million euros."

Janie rolled her eyes.

"C'mon. Give me a break," I laughed again. "There's no way that a coin can be worth one million euros."

"I'm afraid there is," Renard stated.

"But that whole story is bullshit," I blurted out. No one reacted. They all just watched us. "I mean, how on earth can something be so valuable, strictly based on conjecture?"

"The coin is worth whatever anyone would pay for it. That's fundamental. Monsieur Peukington has had many generous offers," Renard said.

"Who has made offers?" Fleuse asked.

"A few museums, several wealthy collectors," Renard answered.

"Well, it's not all conjecture," Pistache said to me, still irked by my question.

"Jacques is right," Renard added. "Plus, the coin has changed so few hands in its time."

"Sorry," Janie interrupted. "I just don't buy it."

"Look at it this way," Renard mused. "The coin's story doesn't matter. I'm going to find it tonight, period. The faster that happens, the sooner that you and your husband can head out on the town."

Part of me was intrigued, but Janie wasn't buying any of the hype. I could already see Fleuse's eyes beginning to wander around the room, searching for the object. Renard and Pistache were focused on me, maybe in part because they believed that I might have already found it before they arrived. Regardless, I was officially curious.

"Okay," I said. "Let's find it."

*   *   *

The bar exploded in motion. The six of us frantically searched. I felt as though I had a distinct advantage in that I was already behind the bar. I was pulling open cupboards and drawers that didn't want to budge, expecting all the while to find the object.

I checked beneath the bust of the man, inside the paned-glass door of the clock, and under every single bottle of liquor. I sifted through cobwebs stretched across the back of the record player. I even patted down the old flannel and checked the insides of the old shoes. I wasn't finding the coin.

"It will never be behind the bar," Pistache exclaimed from under a table. "It's too obvious! You're wasting your time."

It dawned on me that I wouldn't know what to do with the coin if I were the one who found it. One of these people would undoubtedly take it from me whether I wanted to give it up or not. I suppose that I just wanted to know what it felt like to hold an artifact worth one million euros. Maybe Janie and I could get our picture taken with it. No one back home would believe me, but to hold Napoleon's lucky coin in my hand? Normal tourists don't get that kind of experience.

I realized that I'd chosen to believe in the coin's far-fetched history. The story itself was ridiculous, but I pictured retelling friends with as much drama as I could muster. I knew Janie would love that part as well. When my buddies back home expressed their doubts about Napoleon being saved by a single lucky coin, I would simply answer with a shrug and say, "What do you think he was holding when he had his hand in his shirt as he posed for all those paintings?"

"You see it back there?" Janie asked.

"No," I yelled back as I searched the crevices of a particularly cobwebby cabinet.

I caught a glimpse of her out of the corner of my eye. Although entertained by the story, she wasn't working up a sweat to find the object. She'd been writing on a napkin again.

But now as she sat sipping her drink, her eyes giggled at the sight of the room being examined. Chairs and tables were being upended. Pistache was practically fully upside down as he peered into the piano's cavernous shell. Renard looked here and there, all the while keeping an eye on everyone else. He didn't want someone making a dash for the door.

And, Janie sat there spectating. She didn't think I noticed her run her hand along the underside of the bar, an action that betrayed her coolness.

As it all happened, I somehow managed visions of finding the loot and concealing it quickly. I wasn't sure how, but I pictured us getting out of the bar and heading home. The desire to keep the coin in a drawer for years was overwhelming, but thoughts of riches continually danced through my head. I could leave my job at the paper, and Janie and I could travel the world finding spots like the Bon Parisien everywhere.

I was peering into the empty insides of a trophy cup on the shelves behind the bar, when I noticed Janie again. Still casually running her hand beneath the bar, I could tell that she felt something that interested her.

She looked around the room to check for anyone who might be watching her particularly closely, and then casually joined me behind the bar.

"What did you find?" I asked as I wiped cookie jar dust from my hands.

She didn't answer, only knelt to get a better view of the bar's underside. I saw her once again reach for something, and a moment later she was holding an envelope. She placed it on the bar and we looked at it.

The envelope was in pretty decent shape. It wasn't torn, wrinkled, or discolored. It could not have been suspended underneath the bar for very long. Each corner was adorned with the remnants of scotch tape. The tape was also not worn or brittle.

"Is the coin inside?" I asked.

"I don't think so," she answered. "Didn't feel like it."

"Did you find something?" Renard shouted in our direction.

"Probably not," I said. "It's not the coin."

Janie flipped the envelope over, and I felt a pang of excitement shimmy up my spine. Written in marker on the back of the envelope were the words, "Open if I am gone."

"Who wrote that?" Janie asked.

"How should I know?" I answered.

"That's Victor's handwriting," Trudel stated. I hadn't noticed, but she'd joined us. In fact, everyone was now watching Janie and me.

"Well, open it," I urged.

Janie slowly separated the folds of the envelope. She handled it as if she were an archeologist carefully opening scrolls. She pulled out a piece of paper. The handwriting was carelessly scrawled across the page.

Janie read, "If I am dead, blame Trudie."

The room stood quietly as all eyes found Trudel.

"Where did you find that?" she asked.

"It was taped under the bar," Janie answered.

"Well, I have no idea why he would have written that," she defended herself with a shake of her head.

"Probably," Pistache interjected under his breath, "because you're a crazy witch."

Her eyes burned as she looked at him. Fleuse was also gnashing his teeth over the comment, but no one addressed it.

"Is there a date on it?" I asked.

"Nope," Janie responded.

Renard craned his neck to see the note. He was still hovering near the curtain. His wheels were turning as if every word were a clue.

"Well, I don't know what that note is about," Trudel stated matter-of-factly.

"What did you do to him?" Pistache hissed.

"Nothing!"

"Now Jacques," Fleuse began. "That doesn't mean anything yet. It's just a letter."

"Victor must have written it because he saw his own disappearance as a real possibility!" Pistache exclaimed.

"Well, I know," Fleuse said with a pacifying tone. "But ..."

"He was your friend!" Pistache exclaimed. "Doesn't it seem obvious what happened? She got rid of him!"

"I was in love with Victor!" Trudel yelled. "I miss him so much! Why would I kill him?"

Fleuse silently withdrew a little.

"Because," Pistache explained, "you wanted the coin!"

"Not in exchange for Victor!"

"Everybody, hang on," I said. "I know that some of this stuff isn't my business, but this note isn't much to go on. We have no idea when he wrote it, or the context in which he wrote it. Plus, his name isn't even on it anywhere. It would be different if he'd signed it or something."

"Don't be naïve, American!" Pistache blurted out.

"Well, you guys don't know if he's even dead, right?" I countered. "He is just gone. Madame von Hugelstein thinks he's off with another woman!"

"I'd rather he were dead if that were the case," Trudel huffed.

"You don't mean that," Fleuse finally spoke again.

"What's your play, man?" Pistache answered Fleuse. "Are you so taken by this woman that you will defend her no matter what she says? Even if it means your heart is on the line?!"

"Or a million euros?" Renard interjected.

"The American is right, though," Fleuse began. "We don't even know for sure if it's Victor who wrote that!"

"Or whether or not he's dead," I reminded everyone again.

"C'mon," Pistache said with a flick of his wrist. "I need another drink." He approached the bar.

"She said it's his handwriting," Janie pointed out.

As I poured him another, Pistache slumped on a barstool, creating a rush of air that sent the envelope to the floor in a featherlike fall. I bent to retrieve it. Trudel spoke as I crouched.

"Well, I don't know what to tell you all. I certainly didn't do anything to Victor."

"Except play him for a fool and maybe kill him," Pistache grunted.

"Please," she answered.

I barely registered any of their conversation. With envelope in hand, I was about to stand up again when I noticed something peering at me from the darkness beneath the sinks. It was the door to a safe.

"Hey check this out." I put a hand on it to pull it out, but it wouldn't budge.

"What is it?" I heard Janie say.

I shifted my weight. My eyes adjusted to the darkness. The safe was small and very heavy for its size, though not immovable. It's grey rough exterior felt like thick stone. It could fit easily in my arms, but first I would need to brace my legs on something to drag it out from under the bar and into the light.

Janie repeated herself. "C'mon, Pete. What is it?"

"It's a safe," I said with a grunt. It took all the power that my legs could muster, and my back torqued as I hugged it close to my chest and dragged it out of the darkness. With one quick and painful motion, I hoisted it to the bar top. It landed with a thud. For a moment the wood made a "crack" sound beneath the weight of the safe, but nothing was damaged.

"What's inside?" Fleuse asked.

"I have no idea," I said. "Feels like bricks."

"Maybe it's the bar money," Janie said.

"I think it's too small for that," I said. "You'd need more cash on hand to properly run this joint. The hotel probably has a much larger office safe for that kind of stuff. This looks like it's for jewelry or something."

"Or maybe a coin," Pistache said with a glint in his eye.

Instinctively, I lowered my ear to the safe door and turned the dial of the combination lock.

"What are you doing?" Janie asked, laughing.

"I have no idea. Aren't you supposed to hear a little click or something when you pass the correct number?"

Pistache laughed too.

"You watch too many movies," Janie said, smiling.

She was right. I had no clue what I was doing. I don't even know what made me think that was going to work.

"Well, does anyone have the combination?" Fleuse asked.

"I didn't even know that was there," Trudel answered.

We all stared at it for a second.

"Here, I'll tip it back a little and you guys look under it," I offered.

"Why?" asked Janie.

"When I was a kid, I had a safe. There was a sticker on the bottom with the combination on it."

"No way it'll be there," Fleuse muttered quietly.

"Buy me a drink if it is?" Pistache answered him under his breath.

I tipped it back, and Janie shook her head. Nothing.

"Knew it," Fleuse said.

"Sorry, honey," Janie said. "Long shot. This safe isn't a toy."

"My safe wasn't either," I joked. "It legitimately protected my baseball cards."

She rolled her eyes at me.

"How are we going to get it open?" Fleuse asked.

"I bet we can find a way," Pistache uttered with his trademark energy.

"Hang on a second," I said. "We can't do anything that will harm this safe. I know I don't officially work here, but it belongs to the hotel. We can't open it without their permission."

"Listen to you," Pistache smirked. "Afraid it'll be charged to the room?"

"Actually yes," I said with a look toward Janie. "That hadn't occurred to me, but now that you mention it, yes."

"Take it easy," Pistache said as he threw his arms around the object. "There's a lot more at stake here." With one heave, he pulled the safe from the bar. He must have misjudged its weight, because it instantly sent him to the floor beneath the momentum of his action. Pinned to the ground, he groaned. I was not the only one trying to conceal a smile.

"Could someone give me a hand?" he asked from beneath the weight.

Fleuse went to his aid, and they both managed it back to the bar.

"Let's leave it up here," Pistache said, with hurting body and bruised pride.

"Good idea," I snickered.

"So really. How do we open it?" Janie asked.

Chapter XI.

Victor scurried down the sidewalk in the pale Parisian summer evening's light, swerving through pedestrian traffic. The ends of his shoelaces gently tapped the pavement as he ran. Passing several artists painting the great Notre-Dame de Paris, Victor was in too much of a rush to notice their bright depictions of the sunset in front of its twin bell towers.

He'd asked Trudel to meet him somewhere other than the bar, and he was running late. Surely, this turned her off and would add to their recent troubles. Lately, Trudel had grown jealous of anyone who commanded Victor's attention, which was exacerbated by his recent distractions with Fleuse and Jacques.

He knew that Trudel would also be disappointed that he had asked her to meet him at an inside table. Victor didn't think she'd like being kept from the cool natural light that hung in the sky late into the summer evening. But given the sensitive nature of their conversation, the soft yellow of the interior would have to do.

Trudel sat scowling at him when Victor burst through the door of Le Rive Gauche, a long thin café with dirty tiled flooring. There was no chair sitting at the small table across from her.

"Someone asked if I was using it, and I said no. I just assumed you weren't going to be here."

"Okay. Sorry," he answered, out of breath. He glanced around for another chair.

Trudel silently bristled as she sipped on her brandy. Victor snagged a chair from an empty table next to him and craned his neck to see the barista.

"A whiskey, please," he called out.

"Really? What's happening to you?" Trudel asked.

"What?"

"I don't think I've ever seen you drink whiskey."

"I drink it all the time."

"No you don't. I've only seen you drink a beer once and a while in the bar."

The waitress delivered his glass just as Victor reached inside his coat pocket and produced a pouch of tobacco and rolling papers. He quickly downed the spirit.

"Another, please," he said to the woman as he began assembling a cigarette.

"What is this?!" Trudel continued.

"I know, I know. You've never seen me smoke."

"Do I know you at all?"

Victor fussed over his process as he spoke. "I did this much more regularly as a young man."

"You aren't smoking that, you know."

"Why not?" he asked without even looking up, refusing to be interrupted.

"Because you can't smoke that in my face."

"I won't."

"Yes you will. You're going to smoke that right here and I'm not going to be able to keep it away from me."

"Relax."

"I am a singer!" she protested loudly. "Do you have any idea what that could do to my throat?!"

Victor stopped. He had just finished. He made a face and placed the pouch back in his jacket pocket and left his newly rolled cigarette on the table.

"Fine," he said frankly as he set the cigarette next to his empty whiskey glass.

They sat in silence for a brief moment until the waitress brought Victor's second whiskey.

"So," he continued. "How was the show today?"

"Why did you ask me here?" Trudel answered.

Victor picked up the new drink and said, "Can't we just get out of the bar every once and a while? Plus, I have something to show you."

"Are you breaking up with me?" she asked with a sharp tone.

"What? No!"

"Did you bring me here to break up with me? If so, I see what you're doing and it's not going to work."

"What are you talking about? I'm not breaking up with you."

"You want to get me on neutral territory," Trudel accused.

"Trudie. Stop it."

She eyed him suspiciously. "Who is she?"

"Will you please stop it with this. You sound crazy."

"Really? Then it's time to explain yourself." It was her turn to need another drink. She motioned for the waitress before snapping at Victor, "So get on with it. Here I am sitting across from my boyfriend, and he won't even tell me what's going on."

"Okay, okay. I just got here, let me take a second."

"Sure you go ahead with that. Imagine how silly I felt sitting here alone, the weird lady. Plus, I just heard myself say the words 'my boyfriend.' How old am I, anyway? It's embarrassing."

"What would you prefer to call me?"

She didn't answer. She just took a sip of her newly delivered drink.

Victor followed suit. After quickly draining his second glass he shifted in his chair momentarily.

"Like I said before your tirade just now, I have something to show you." He pulled a small box out of his jacket pocket.

"It wasn't a tirade," she began until she saw the object. Trudel gasped. "What's that?!"

"Oh, just a little something that I've run across."

Trudel seized the tiny package. "Oh, Victor!"

He was a little uneasy with how quickly she nabbed it from him. Still, he reminded himself that it was highly unlikely that Trudel would just up and run off with it.

"It's not wrapped," she muttered as she removed the top. "Huh. A coin?"

"Well, it's not just any …"

"What the hell am I going to do with a coin?"

"What? What do you mean you?"

Trudel was silent. She looked at him and blinked.

"It's not for you!" Victor continued.

"Oh," she processed. "Why would you give it to me?"

"I didn't. You just grabbed it. I'm showing you." Victor said, snatching it back.

"Oh well, why would I care about that?" She grunted and took a drink.

"Well, it's an exciting coin. It's extremely valuable."

"Do I look like I care about coins?" she snapped.

"I bet that you've never seen a coin like this one, though," Victor said, forgetting about Trudel's misunderstanding.

Barely believing what she heard, Trudel paused a moment before saying, "You know what? I have to go." She swallowed the last of her brandy with one gulp and stood to leave.

"Wait a sec, Trudie! What's the matter with you?" he protested as she was turning to leave.

Trudel immediately pivoted toward him. "You're a dick, that's my problem."

"Take it easy. Sit down. Let me buy you one."

She just stood and stared at him.

He continued, "I'm sorry that I didn't pay you more attention just now. When I walked in, my head was spinning. Let me make it up to you now."

Trudel bit her lip, blinked three times rapidly, and sat down again. "I'll have just one more," she finally conceded.

"Good. Thank you."

"So what is the story about your coin?"

"Well, really it is the key to my retirement."

"Is that so?"

"Yes, madame," Victor stated proudly.

"I don't follow," she deadpanned.

"Well once I get this thing moved off I won't have to work in the bar, for starters."

She put her glass down and looked at him. "How can something that small possibly be that valuable?"

"Oh, it is."

"So what then? What will you do when you don't work in the bar?" Trudel asked.

Victor wondered for a moment, smiling. "I'm thinking move down south. Enjoy the sun for a while."

"The Riviera? Are you serious?"

"Absolutely," he said with another drink.

"Well, where would I sing?"

"What do you mean?"

"I can't leave! I am too attached to my theatre. How do you think my fans would react?"

"Wait, you'd want to come along?"

"Well, that's what you're saying, isn't it?"

"Sure." Victor tried to cover his tracks. It hadn't occurred to him to invite Trudel.

"You weren't going to invite me?!" She shouted as she rose grandly.

"Of course I was, that's what I'm doing now!" Victor answered, lying.

Trudel turned to leave again. "I don't know why I put myself through this kind of thing," she huffed as she rifled through her purse to find money for her drinks. "It's always the same with you. I come in to the bar, you don't get around to talking with me for thirty minutes these days, and even then you're distracted."

"I'm at work when that happens."

"You are always more interested in other women than you are in me, and here is another instance when I am not a priority for you!"

"Those other people in the bar are actual patrons. Would you take it easy?" He too stood and reached for her arm, but she slapped his hand away.

"Don't touch me!" she snapped. The baristas were now beginning to notice the behavior from the table.

"Okay. Hang on. Don't go," Victor said with renewed calmness. "Please, let me start over with this."

"I'll give you five minutes. Start making sense."

"Great, thank you."

"After that," she said as she sat down, "I'm going to find somewhere to enjoy the evening outside without you."

"Yes, great. Thank you. Actually I do have to apologize," Victor explained as they both sat again. He shot a reassuring look toward the café employees as he spoke. "I chose to sit inside for a reason."

"Why?"

"Well, it's the coin. It is very valuable."

"Yes, you said that."

"No Trudie, you don't understand. It's really valuable."

"Okay?"

"I haven't even told Fleuse or Jacques, yet," the bartender admitted.

"Fleuse? What does he have to do with anything?"

"Well, he brought it to me. Apparently his friend, Jacques, is the one who first got the coin."

Trudel thought for a moment. "Jacques? I don't remember a friend of Fleuse's named Jacques. Actually, I'm not sure that I even remember him being mentioned."

"Trust me," Victor said with a sip. "You would remember this guy. He's an impressionist."

"I hate impressionists."

"I told them you would."

"Okay, continue," she said with a sigh.

"Well, these guys bring me this coin, because they know that I'm into this stuff. Only thing is, they have no idea how much it is worth."

"And you haven't told them?"

"Well, I myself didn't know at the time either. I had to take it to the collectors shop to get it appraised. I haven't met with them yet on it."

"So how much is it worth? I didn't know that you could move to the South of France because of the price of one coin."

"Well, this is no ordinary collectible. As a coin itself, it's already valuable. I was glad to hear the initial estimates, but I did some digging of my own. See, this particular coin has had articles written about it, files kept on it. It's the stuff of lore."

*   *   *

Over several more drinks, Victor laid out the entire story for Trudel. He detailed everything from the coin itself to Peukington's family. When it was finally over, they sat in silence for almost an entire minute. With the warmth of multiple drinks and fresh cocktails in front of them, Trudel finally broke the quiet.

"Fleuse is going to be thrilled," she said. "Are you going to split it all evenly?"

Victor took a sip and shifted. "We haven't really spoken about it yet."

"Well that's important, don't you think? What if they want to give you less?"

"They won't." Victor didn't believe himself as he said it. He had known Fleuse for a long time, but his new friend Jacques wasn't a trustworthy person.

"So when are you planning on seeing them next?"

"They are going to stop in tomorrow on my next shift. They don't know that I've had it appraised already. They think that it's going to happen tomorrow morning."

"Why didn't you tell them?"

"Well, at first I was going to immediately. I called off the first part of my shift today just to be able to get it done early. I was curious."

"So why didn't you go running to them with the good news?"

"Well, I wanted to be able to do a little digging on my own. The appraiser mentioned in passing the Napoleon story. He didn't think it was really the coin, but I didn't tell him it came from Peukington, either."

"I see. How are you going to sell the coin?"

"I'm not sure yet."

"What if Lavaar Peukington comes looking for it? He's not the kind of person who'd be understanding about any of this."

"Isn't that the truth?" Victor said with a laugh. "I'm thinking that we'll all take turns holding it. That way, if someone is suspected, he may not have it on him."

"You could always give it to me to hold," Trudel said with a casual shrug of the shoulders.

Victor snickered. "Sure." He took another drink.

"Don't laugh about it! Why is that so crazy?!" Trudel bristled again.

"You were serious? Why would I give it to you?"

"Obviously you can trust me! I would never be suspected by Peukington!"

She had a point. As his girlfriend, she wouldn't be entirely beyond suspicion, but Trudel was removed from the situation even more than he was. Still, he was not sure if he were truly able to trust her. Their relationship was not always perfect, and Victor worried what might happen if they experienced one of their fights while she had the coin.

"I can't believe it's taking you this long to think it over," Trudel said.

"Sorry. Truth is, I'd pretty much assumed that I'd stash it in the bar somewhere for safe keeping."

"The bar?! Why there?"

"Well, I don't want it in my home, do I?"

Trudel shrugged and took a drink.

"I mean, I don't need someone like Peukington in my house," Victor continued. "There would be plenty of places in the bar to hide it. I'm there all the time, anyway."

"Like where in the bar?"

"I don't know. There are tons of places." Victor had actually already considered many specific hiding places in the bar. He wasn't about to tell Trudel, though.

"I think I've heard enough." Trudel stood and collected her purse from the back of the chair.

"What's that supposed to mean?" Victor asked.

"Have a nice time down south."

"What? Are you mad or something?"

"Victor, you have never put my needs first."

"We haven't even been going out that long!"

"You are one selfish prick. I hope that thing is a bad penny and only brings you bad luck." Trudel started to walk away.

Victor finally stood. "Where is this coming from?"

Trudel turned back to him. "You ask me here to tell me your plans for the future. They don't seem to include me. Good luck with whatever hussy you wind up with next."

"Another hussy?! There's only you!"

"Are you calling me a hussy?!"

"What? No! You're crazy. There's no one else!"

Trudel had reached the door. Without turning she said, "Yeah, yeah, there's always some hussy!"

She was gone.

Victor stayed in the café for a good while longer. As baristas meandered by over the next hour or so, he sheepishly made eye contact just long enough to indicate the need for another drink. In hindsight, he considered it a mistake telling Trudel about the coin.

Victor had also thought of withholding the coin's worth from Fleuse and Jacques. As he sat and drank, he weighed his options. He had ruled out giving the coin to Trudel to hide, but he realized the potential in leaving town. The others would likely never find him.

Chapter XII.

The safe hit the crimson carpet with a thud.

"Nope," Fleuse said dryly.

"Can you get any higher?" Renard asked me.

Already standing on the bar, I searched for another avenue. "Well, this is about the highest point in the room for me to stand on," I replied. "What if we try to hit it with something?"

"Pistache, drink," I heard Janie say as she threw an ace down. A casual game had begun anew when it became obvious that six people were too many to try and open a safe. I found it a little funny that I could not discern whether or not Janie said the word "Pistache" because she played the ace or she was telling Pistache to take a drink. I peeked out of the corner of my eye to realize that it was both.

Pistache was actively helping us with suggestions here and there, but it was apparent that this guy could not resist a good drinking game.

"Spades," he muttered, taking a swig of his latest cocktail before offering us a new idea. "The leg of a chair might work well as a kind of lever on the combination dial."

Willing to try anything, we agreed. Renard sat the safe upright, and tilted a chair against it.

"This is not going to work," Trudel muttered before playing the two of spades.

"Here goes," Renard said simply as he thrust his foot on to the seat of the chair. A sharp crack sounded loudly as one of the legs of the chair splintered and a nail pulled away from its framework. It was a good effort, but the safe was knocked backwards and the chair upended.

"Hmm," Renard thought out loud.

"Note to self," Pistache said without looking up. "Don't sit in that chair."

"So, Jacques," Janie asked.

"Yes?" the pickpocket answered.

"Show me a trick."

"What do you mean?"

"You know, one of your sneaky 'get someone's watch' magic tricks," she said as she played a card.

"He's not a magician!" Renard shouted from across the room as he made another awkward attempt with the chair on the safe's door.

"Ah, I see," Pistache answered. "You are looking for some sleight of hand."

"Exactly."

"A magician ..." Pistache glanced at Renard who again looked our direction, "I mean pickpocket, never reveals his secrets."

"Oh come on," she said as the game continued. "We're all friends here."

"We are?" Trudel asked.

"Well we are after all this," I muttered.

"Sorry, ma cherie," Pistache said to Janie.

"Just go ahead, Pistache," Renard chimed in again from his spot with the safe. "She'll get a kick out of it. Haven't you been trying to impress her all evening?"

"It's true," Janie added flirtatiously. "I'll be impressed."

Pistache looked at me. I shrugged. He was annoying, but Janie was flirting with this guy whether I liked it or not. I threw some whiskey in a glass and downed it immediately.

"Ok, I'll teach you one thing," he said, sighing.

"Excellent," she said as she put her cards down.

I heard another leg splinter from the chair.

"It's called the Sailor's Revenge," Pistache explained.

"Okay," Janie answered. "What is it, and why is it called that?"

"Well, it's said that sailors developed it to lift the key to the rum cabinet."

"At least it has a cool name."

"It's pretty simple, really. But, it takes a lot of practice. Watch closely." The pickpocket turned to me. "Would you hand me a bottle cap?"

Plenty of beer bottle caps were lying around. I immediately found one on the floor behind the bar.

"You see," he continued, nabbing the item from me. "You pick up the object with your thumb and forefinger and close the rest of your fingers around it, like this."

I handed Janie a second bottle cap. The game of Pistache had been momentarily suspended.

"Got it, that's easy enough," she said, mimicking his actions.

"Good. Now as you turn your fist, work the item between your middle and ring fingers. You'll want to move it through them, to the back of your hand, pinning it with the backs of those fingers. Simultaneously open your hand, exposing your empty palm." As he described it, he opened his fist and spread his fingers apart. The bottle cap had vanished.

"That's a good trick," I marveled.

Janie tried it, and noisily dropped the bottle cap instantly.

Pistache smiled. "Kind of. Relax your hand more," Pistache advised.

She tried it again, this time using her other hand to try and steady the object. "I don't get how you do it so fast," she noted.

"Ah, ah, ah. Don't use your other hand. You never want to get in the habit of trying to rely on it. Someone will always be looking at your other hand. I told you it takes practice."

Janie dropped the bottle cap again.

"The key is to perform it in one fluid motion," Pistache went on. "If your hand stays moving, no one will be able to stay focused on the sleight of hand. That way, even if a corner of the bottle cap is peaking through your fingers, it will be hard to see."

Janie dropped the bottle cap yet again. "I'm not getting it."

"Well, I didn't say it was easy, ma cherie."

Again, the chair splintered under the weight of another awkward attempt at opening the safe.

"That didn't work," Fleuse muttered the obvious to Renard as he gazed at the situation.

"That's true, Monsieur Newman," Renard answered through his teeth. "Thank you."

"I am going to need another beer," Pistache said with disappointment as he moved on from the sleight-of-hand trick. The game was burning through drinks.

Janie was still transfixed on the bottle cap without showing any signs of improvement.

"Wait a minute," the pickpocket asked me. "Can you make a Feu du Saint Denis?"

"I have no idea what that is," I answered.

"It's a flavored whiskey shot, and the top of it is on fire."

"Who was Saint Denis?" I asked.

"He was a saint."

"Huh, okay. Let's try and keep the lighting of fires to an absolute minimum," I responsibly suggested. As a bartender in college, I was familiar with making drinks like these. They're hard to get right, not to mention dangerous.

"Well, think about it," Pistache persisted. "What if there was a way to somehow use the fire to open the safe?"

Everyone was attentive. I didn't like the idea of lighting a fire, but with one million euros at stake, I figured I couldn't stop the pickpocket.

"I can't believe I'm still playing this game," Trudel muttered. She had never put down her cards. No one paid any attention.

"That's a terrible idea," Renard sounded as the voice of reason. He apparently didn't want any fire in the bar either. He was too busy setting up the scene for another go with a chair. He was putting more care into it this time though as he searched for the exact angle for proper leverage.

"It's not such a bad idea!" Pistache disagreed. "Maybe we weaken something that can give way in the lock."

"Or we wind up melting it shut," Fleuse offered. He still stood with Renard and the chair.

"Fleuse is right," Trudel offered.

"Thank you," Fleuse said, touched by the attention from Trudel.

"Well for whatever it's worth, I don't love it either," Janie added.

Pistache scoffed. "Go back to working on your bottle cap trick." He nodded in Janie's direction, but spoke next to Trudel. "Keep your friend quiet."

Janie gave him a little scowl and threw the small metal item at him lightly. He didn't react.

"Take it easy, Jacques," Fleuse said in defense of the ladies.

"Bite me, Fleuse. I can take care of myself," Trudel spat.

"Well," Pistache continued, "it looks like your chair thing is working really well, so maybe you should keep going with that while I make a Feu du Saint Denis for everyone here who likes me."

"Let's just hear him out for a second," Fleuse said to Renard after a moment of reconsideration. He turned back to Pistache. "Ok Jacques, what do you propose?"

Pistache looked my way. "Do you mind if I join you?"

"No, come on back."

He scurried around the bar and joined me. Snagging a bottle of whiskey, he carelessly swung it from the shelf. "Let's see," he wondered aloud. "Do you see any poison du poisson?"

"I have never heard of that, either."

"It's serious stuff," Fleuse interjected.

"He's right," Pistache answered, standing on his toes to search the liquor bottles. "It's a spirit extracted from a fish only found in the Mediterranean. It's the highest-proof liquor there is. Just a dash is perfect for this drink, but even as much as a shot of poison du poisson straight up will cause memory blackouts almost immediately."

"It's said that you wouldn't be able to walk within the hour," Fleuse added, hands in pockets.

Janie's eyes widened as she shook her head at me.

"Maybe we should steer clear of that stuff, then," I suggested.

"Found it!" Pistache exclaimed.

He pulled a dusty bottle from the back of the shelves. Dark amber liquor sloshed inside as he set it on the bar.

"Why would anyone have that around if it's so dangerous?" I wondered.

"A lot of people like the Feu du Saint Denis, American," the pickpocket answered. "Can't make one without this. It really looks and smells about like regular whiskey. It's illegal in the United States, you know."

"Is there at least a warning on the label?"

"You worry too much," Pistache said.

Another thud.

"We need a big hammer," Renard said, having just tried dropping the safe again. "Is there a tool chest anywhere back there?"

"I have not seen one," I replied as I picked up the bottle of poison du poisson as Jacques set up shot glasses. He was right. It smelled just like ordinary whiskey, which fueled my fear of the drink.

"I never saw Victor back there with a hammer or tools," Trudel added. "Pistache, young lady."

Janie took a sip of her drink. "Diamonds," she countered.

"Ah, here we go!" Pistache exclaimed as he flipped a bottle in his hand.

"Now the trick with these," Pistache said as he grabbed the bottle from me and began mixing, "is to gently trickle the high proof alcohol over the top. Just a touch only. This way, it lights easier because it has not mixed completely into the body of the drink." With that, he struck a match and whisked it across the row of drinks with a dramatic flare. Each one glowed a gentle purple flame. "The flavor will be there after the burn."

"Yeah, that's great, but I agree with Monsieur Renard," I said. "I don't think this will help us with the safe. You could do more damage than good. What if something melts?"

Pistache didn't have a good answer. He picked up one of the shot glasses, blew the tiny fire out, and drank it.

"You know what we could do," Fleuse interjected. "How about we run an experiment?"

"Somebody do these with me before they burn out," Pistache said barely listening. Fleuse walked to the bar. Everyone except Renard grabbed a shot glass. Janie stared into hers distrustfully.

Reassuring her, I said, "I know from making drinks like these that the flame burns off the high-proof stuff. It's been going long enough now. We're okay."

"I'm just trying to avoid waking up naked in a park," she joked.

"Which park are you thinking?" Pistache asked, smiling.

We all blew out the flame, and drank the contents.

"So what kind of experiment?" Janie asked Fleuse as she placed the empty shot glass on the bar with a knock sound.

"Yeah, I don't follow," Pistache said.

"Let's see just how hot this booze burns and its effect on intricate metalwork," Fleuse suggested. "We might be able to tell if it will cause more harm than good. We can use my watch."

"You don't want to do that," I warned. "It'll probably trash it."

"Yeah, I bet you built that, right?" Trudel added.

"No," Fleuse said with a smile as he unfastened the wristband. "I make clocks. This is an inexpensive little thing. Funny, isn't it?"

As Fleuse began to unlatch his watch's wristband, Janie was craning her neck to see.

"What do you think, my dear?" I asked.

"I don't know. This could work," she answered.

"Pistache again, young lady," Trudel said to Janie.

Janie continued after taking a sip. "Maybe the gears of the watch will melt and shrink up. Once properly cooled, they might become brittle. I don't know. I just want to see it happen. This could work."

"Yeah, I guess," I said.

"Honestly, I wouldn't mind seeing it fail, either. Melting a watch might be pretty cool to see."

Fleuse laid his timepiece out on the bar, and Pistache carelessly splashed booze on top of it. It was way more than necessary. Before a split second had passed, the watch was lying in a full-fledged puddle of alcohol on the bar.

"Okay, hang on," I said. "You can't light that now. You'll ignite the whole place."

"So?" Pistache said with laugh, sounding reckless.

"Wait a sec," I said. I reached for a bar rag and started running water in one of the sinks. I at least wanted to have a damp towel on hand and a basin filled with water. "Let me just be prepared for something to go wrong."

Another thud. I looked up to see Renard standing on a chair, staring down at the safe on the ground.

"You're so good, baby," Janie said.

"Is there a fire extinguisher back here?" I asked myself. I hadn't seen one when I was searching earlier.

"Now you're just being ridiculous. We won't need one," Pistache said.

"Well, I don't know. The last thing I need to be is the American who burned down Paris' best little bar."

"Just soak more than one towel," Janie offered. "I'm sure we'll be fine."

"That's a good idea. Back up, Pistache."

Trudel and Janie took a sip. I was quietly amused by their Pavlovian response to the pickpocket's name. I blotted some of the excess booze.

"Well, don't clean it all up," Pistache protested. "We'll need a good and hot situation here."

I huffed. I was convinced that he was willing to burn the entire place down.

"Ready?" Pistache continued.

"Okay, I guess," I answered, backing away a little.

With great flare, a match was lit and dropped on Fleuse's watch and an audible "poof" accompanied its envelopment in flame. As I predicted, the fire extended to the bar top itself. The wood wasn't burning, but I was instantly uneasy about it anyway. As the liquor allowed the flame to dance about half an inch above the bar, Fleuse's watch started to change color.

"Ah!" Pistache exclaimed, loving the spectacle.

Janie leaned in to get a better look at the situation. It had only been a few short seconds, but I was nervous.

"Okay that's enough," I said. "Should be plenty."

I thrust a towel over the watch and began to corral the flame. It worked to suppress it, but I grabbed a second rag from the sink and threw it on top as well.

"Hey!" Pistache said. "It wasn't done yet!" In an instant, he grabbed the towels and threw them back at me. He then turned the bottle upside down over the tiny flame and doused the nearly extinguished ash with more booze. The entire surface of the bar directly in front of me jumped with flame.

"Jesus!" I exclaimed as I grabbed the last of the soaking towels and threw them on the bar. I squeezed all the water out to counteract the copious amount of spilled liquor, but found myself with outstretched arms trying to cover the entire surface area of burning material.

"Ha ha!" Pistache yelled as his eyes danced over his work. Janie and Trudel jumped up with matching exclamations of terror.

"Are you crazy?!" I yelled as I worked myself between him and the mini-blaze. I was suppressing much of the flame, but quickly noticed that the sleeve of my shirt was now part of the small inferno.

"Honey, your arm!" Janie yelled.

I hadn't felt it yet. I instinctively thrust my arm into the filled sink. When I brought it out, I splashed excess water on the bar. Finally, I didn't see any more flames.

"Are you okay?" Janie asked.

"Smooth, Jacques," Fleuse muttered sarcastically.

"Did I get it all?" I asked as I recovered from the panic.

"What happened to the watch?" Pistache asked.

"Are you kidding right now?!" I erupted. "Give me that!" I yelled as I yanked the bottle of liquor out of his hand. "Get out from behind here!" I forcibly grabbed his collar and dragged him out from behind the bar. A little too drunk to stand his ground, he was easy to remove. "What is the matter with you, Pistache?" I yelled.

Janie and Trudel took a sip.

"Okay, Pierre. Take it easy," Pistache said, defending himself only a little. "I just wanted to see what happened to the watch!"

"Honey, is your arm okay?" Janie repeated as she came to me to inspect the damage.

"No, it's fine. I didn't feel anything. It was just the shirt and the alcohol burning. It only lasted a split second." I took a moment to look down at my arm. My favorite blue plaid shirt was missing a cuff and was singed mostly black from the upper right arm down. Plus, most of it was soaking wet from the extinguishing efforts.

"Your favorite shirt," Janie said out loud as she felt the burned edges of the sleeve.

"I think you've improved it," Trudel said with a smirk. "American fashion, hmph!"

"Well, maybe something at least informative came out of this," I said, shaking the wetness from my new half-sleeve. "What does the watch look like?"

Everyone leaned in. The glass was no longer clear but covered in a brown fog. The band itself was badly burned. The face wasn't even visible anymore.

"Looks like it's ruined," Trudel observed.

"I just don't see how this is going to help with the safe," Janie added.

Renard joined the group to peer at the charred timepiece. "Yeah, we won't be able to do much with that. That was probably a nowhere road to head down anyway. Way to go, Pistache."

Janie and Trudel took a sip.

"And you just stood by and let us do that?!" I furiously asked. "If you knew it was such a bad idea, why didn't you say something?"

Renard looked to the Fleuse. "Would this guy have listened to any objection? Truly?"

"No," Fleuse answered.

I was losing patience. "Okay, let me get this straight. So we just lit this joint on fire, the safe still isn't even open, we have this cryptic letter, and no one really knows at all if the coin is even in here?"

"It's in here," Renard said.

"I mean, do we really know that? So far, I haven't heard any actual evidence that it's here," I shouted.

"No, it's in here," Renard reiterated.

"And what about this lady?" Pistache interjected, as he pointed to the opera singer.

"What about me?!" Trudel exclaimed.

"Well, where's Victor?" he persisted. "I don't know what you did to him, but what if he had the coin on him when you dumped his body?!"

"I didn't dump his body!" Trudel yelled.

"But you killed him!" Pistache answered.

"I did not! Just because some bullshit note pops up doesn't mean that I actually did anything!"

"Then why would he write the note at all?" Pistache continued.

"Well, listen. We weren't the perfect couple, okay? We've had some ups and downs." Trudel looked at Janie and me. "You guys probably know what it's like. Tell them."

We looked at each other. "Maybe," I said skeptically. "I guess we've had disagreements."

Janie shook her head. "We have never fought so much that Pete has felt the need to send a message from beyond the grave to blame me for his disappearance, though."

"Exactly," I confirmed.

"What did you do to him, woman?" Pistache hissed.

"Nothing!" She yelled.

"Take it easy, Jacques," Fleuse defended her.

"And look at you!" Pistache turned his wrath to Fleuse. "You'll be her knight in shining armor at all costs, won't you? It doesn't matter that she killed your long-time friend and lost the key to a world of riches and retirement!"

"I didn't kill him!" Trudel yelled again.

"She didn't!" Fleuse joined in. "Victor is probably out with some woman, like she said!"

"You take that back!" Trudel spat at him. "Victor is a good man!"

"A good man who you think might have taken off with the coin and left you?!" Pistache yelled. "Sounds like a motive for murder to me!"

I finally noticed Trudel starting to cry a little. Janie and I didn't know what to make of it. Before I had the chance to try and settle the situation down, Renard again stepped forward.

"Okay everyone," he began. "It's time to calm down. This conversation is helping no one."

Pistache didn't appreciate Renard's efforts to pacify the group. "What does any of this matter to you other than the coin itself? You're just some rich guy's lackey."

"You're right," Renard answered calmly. "At least about part of that. I don't care about you guys shouting at each other, but I do care about finding this coin. So can everyone please focus and get back to helping me get this safe open?"

"Why should we?" Pistache asked. "Truly. Why would we do that? If it's in there, you're just going to run off with it. Besides, this American idiot is right. How do we even know that the coin is here in the bar?"

"It is," he said.

"C'mon," Pistache huffed. "How can you be so sure?"

"Because," Renard said with a sigh, "Victor didn't have it with him when he left this bar for the last time. I've been pretty careful about this. I've tracked it up until here, and I don't think it's gone anywhere."

"How do you know that Victor didn't have it on him for his last shift?" Fleuse asked.

Renard took a deep breath. "Listen. Everyone stay calm when I say this. You've been going on and on for the last few minutes about this poor woman and the old bartender."

Trudel wiped the tears from her eyes with a dirty napkin.

Renard continued. "She didn't kill Victor Laquer. It's time to take it easy on her."

"How do you know that?" Pistache hissed.

"I know that Victor hasn't run off with another woman, and I know that he didn't have the coin."

"How?" Trudel asked.

"He's dead," Renard uttered bluntly. "And I'm the one who killed him."

Chapter XIII.

Victor Laquer emerged from the Hôtel des Bretons into the cool dark air. It was almost three in the morning, and the Rue de l'Échelle was quiet. Another shift was finished in the bar.

Two weeks had passed since the bartender told Fleuse and Pistache about the worth of the coin. The two men were ecstatic at the value of the piece, and Victor was happy that he'd decided to tell them. The three men toasted each other and their futures. They planned to hide the coin together until they could sell it, but Victor was beginning to feel a creeping uneasiness.

No one had come looking for the coin. So far, the lack of consequences bothered the bartender. Why hadn't Peukington hunted them down? Silence on his strolls home made Victor uncomfortable. A walk that was once treasured and charming was now haunting. Victor tried to convince himself that he was simply paranoid.

All of this weighing heavily on his mind, Victor turned into the blackness of the Tuileries. The bartender couldn't ever remember it feeling this dark. His trek felt longer than it really was, he thought. Passages through the gardens were empty, but the bartender caught himself peering into them as he passed. He knew his imagination was getting the best of him.

Victor tried to distract himself with better thoughts, such as the riches of the coin. Even with a balanced split with Fleuse and Jacques, he would have enough to live out the rest of his days without being a bartender.

Victor was sure that Pistache would be broke quickly, even after his share. Fleuse would probably manage it well at first, but even he would likely spend the sum on something foolish. Victor thought the clockmaker would probably spend it all on a woman, likely an unrequited love.

Again, he noticed the silence.

A cab pulled up ahead and a few tourists spilled out. Their drunken laughter rung in the night's silence and tore him from his reverie. He walked briskly toward them. They stood laughing on the sidewalk as one paid the driver.

Victor glided through them as they parted like a school of fish. The group seemed otherwise oblivious to him. Victor noted their lack of awareness and cursed quietly under his breath. He was starting to hate drunken people.

The bartender began across the Pont Royal. As he glanced up the river in the direction of the Île de la Cité, his peripheral vision caught a glimpse of someone turning onto the bridge behind him. Normally, he wouldn't have taken note, but he'd seen this person among the tourists only moments earlier.

The stranger had broken away from the crowd and seemed to be following Victor. The bartender was uneasy. Why would someone take a taxi only to walk another few blocks? After a moment of reflection, Victor realized he couldn't actually remember if the man had emerged from the cab or not. Had this man been waiting for him on the sidewalk all along?

Forgetting the mysterious figure was not easy, even as he turned the corner off the bridge and the stranger disappeared. Victor tried to calm his paranoia. Perhaps this was just another pedestrian.

The bartender glanced back as he trotted across the cobblestoned side street, heading for another turn. Alarmingly, the man had also turned the corner off the bridge behind him and was closer than before.

Victor stopped beneath a streetlight. He wouldn't allow his imagination to run away. If this stranger was in fact following him, it was better to confront this person now. The darkness of narrow streets would not do.

The man's gait immediately lessened, and he smiled at Victor as he approached.

"Victor Laquer?" the stranger asked.

"Yes."

"Julian Renard."

"Okay," Victor answered without expression.

"It's certainly a pleasure to finally meet you." Julian extended his hand.

"Are we supposed to know each other?" Victor answered, motionless.

"Not exactly."

"Okay?" Victor was stumped.

"You are the bartender in the Bon Parisien, no?"

"I am."

"I thought it was you. When I saw you walking, I just had to say something."

"It's very late," Victor noted.

"The thing is," Renard continued affably, "I was in there last week, and I lost a coin."

The bartender shifted nervously.

"It's not worth much of anything," Renard continued. "But it's a little rare, and it's kind of been my lucky penny. You haven't seen it have you? I would have come to the bar, but I just saw you walking by. I haven't made it in yet."

"Haven't seen it," Victor grunted.

"Are you sure? There were two other men in there when I was visiting. Maybe one of them found it?"

"Like I said, sorry. Haven't seen it," Victor said, turning away.

Suddenly, he felt the intense grip of Renard's hand on his cuff. Victor looked back, only to find a very different expression. All kindness was gone.

"Victor. Are you sure that you'd like to proceed this way?"

The bartender's eyes narrowed. "Get your hands off me."

In one swift motion, Renard twisted Victor's wrist behind his back and pinned him to the lamppost. The bartender winced but didn't have enough time to actually make a sound.

"I'm giving you a chance Victor, an out. This is a free pass. Where is it?"

"Are you with Peukington?!" Victor exclaimed in agony. His wrist was beginning to burn, and the cold steel of the streetlamp pressed into his jaw. As he spoke, Renard was rifling through each of his pockets. "Help!" Victor exclaimed, though short of breath. Renard quickly silenced him with his free hand.

"Listen, you are making this harder than it has to be. You obviously don't have the coin on you. I'm about to let go of you. Do you think that we can have a conversation like grown men?"

Victor nodded.

"Fantastic," Renard said, releasing him.

Victor shook his wrist.

"Now, just tell me where it is," Renard continued.

The bartender realized that he had two options. He could confess, and implicate both Fleuse and Jacques, or he could keep lying. If Renard never found the coin, Victor would still have a chance of retiring.

"Who are you?" Victor grunted.

"Again, I'm Julian Renard. Obviously, I am looking for the coin you stole."

"I didn't steal any coin."

"Blah, blah, blah. Victor, I don't know why you're covering for these guys."

"I don't know who you are talking about."

Renard raised his voice. "I'm talking about Jacques Pistache and Fleuse Newman, obviously!"

Victor was alarmed that he knew their names. "Have you been following me?"

"I have. Not for very long, though. I needed to get you completely alone and give you a chance to come clean."

"Why would you give me that chance?"

"Of the three of you, you're smart enough do the right thing. Let's just get this resolved."

"You don't know me."

"Well, I think I do. You're not a criminal, Victor. You are a former accountant, a real professional. You are not the awkward pretender that Fleuse is, and you are certainly not the outright fraud that Jacques is. You're a good guy. Why would you put yourself in such trouble?"

"I don't have it."

Renard paused and seemed to relax a little bit. "Excellent. I already know that but still, excellent. We are making a little progress now."

Victor stared back at him. "How is that progress?"

"Well, you are admitting that you know of a coin."

"No I'm not."

Renard continued, "But you know where it is, no?"

"I don't know what you're talking about," the bartender said defiantly, committing to his lie. He turned to leave.

Peukington's man paused in disappointment before dashing after him.

"That's a shame," Renard persisted as they walked. "Monsieur Peukington will be very unhappy to hear that. You do know who he is, don't you?"

Victor remained silent as they walked, not exactly knowing where to go. He wanted to get safely home but didn't want to lead Renard to his apartment.

Peukington's man continued, "He's a man who knows exactly what he wants. Do you know what you want, Victor Laquer?" Renard asked as he tried to keep pace with Victor. "Really think long and carefully about the next thing you tell me. A misleading statement might set off a chain of events that you can't stop."

The bartender walked on, expressionless.

Renard continued. "We'll be everywhere. We'll be in your bar. We'll be with you on your walk home. We'll be in your apartment. And most of all, we'll be with Trudel."

Victor stopped. Renard knew much more than the bartender had expected.

"What does Trudel have to do with this?" Victor asked.

"You don't think that you've brought her into the situation? When something like this happens, we do not only approach the thief, but we also find anyone they might trust."

"I don't trust Trudel," Victor responded quickly.

Renard snickered. "Having a lover's spat?"

The bartender ground his teeth. "What did Fleuse and Jacques say when you approached them?"

"I haven't yet," Renard answered, stepping in front of the bartender.

For the first time, Victor noticed how much taller Renard was than he.

Peukington's man continued, "Like I said, I'm here to give you the first chance to come clean."

Victor again tried to move around Renard, but this time the man calmly extended a hand and stopped Victor from walking away.

"I am going to be completely honest with you. Are you ready to listen?" Peukington's man said calmly.

Victor nodded with resignation.

"Good," Renard began. "I know how much that coin is worth, and I can guess how much it means to you. I think that we could help each other in this endeavor."

"How so?"

"Well, consider that I might be willing to make sure that you are still compensated if you help me get the coin back from those two monkeys."

Victor remained silent.

"What would you do if I told you that you could still retire? Is it safe to say that was included in your plans?"

Victor raised an eyebrow.

"You won't have to be associated with guys like Fleuse and Jacques anymore. If Trudel is starting to get under your skin, then you can forget about her as well. Or, you could marry her and never worry about life again. I don't care. But, we are willing to help you get there. You will just have to help us first."

"Why would you offer anything like this to me?" the bartender asked.

"Victor," Renard still sounded relaxed. "I am a big fan of peaceful resolutions."

"Could've fooled me," the bartender snickered, touching his sore wrist.

"Right. Sorry about that. Can you blame me, though? The coin is worth a lot and you weren't exactly making things easy for me."

"Why should I believe you? How do I know that you won't just get the coin and leave me high and dry?"

"Because like me, Monsieur Peukington is true to his word."

"Really? I've heard he's cutthroat," Victor said doubtfully.

"I guess that you will just have to trust me. Ask yourself, can you really afford not to?"

Victor stood in silence, thinking.

Renard continued, "Do you really want to roll the dice on your future and safety any more than you already have? How about Trudel's?"

Victor remained silent.

"No one has to get hurt here," Renard continued. "Just give me what I want. All you have to do is tell me where the coin is."

Victor took a deep breath. After his involvement with stealing and hiding the coin, he didn't truly believe that Renard would honor their deal. Plus, Fleuse and Jacques trusted the bartender from the beginning. He hadn't betrayed them before, even though he'd weighed the option, so he wasn't about to do it now.

Victor broke out in a dead sprint.

"Victor!" Renard shouted angrily, watching him run for a moment. "Where are you going?! Haven't I made it clear enough that you have nowhere to go?!"

Victor's mind raced. He knew that he couldn't outrun the man for long, so he tried to reach a more public place. He dashed up a stairway along the river, figuring there might be others on the bridge. Hearing Renard's footsteps closing in, he was disappointed when he reached the top and saw no one.

As he continued running over the bridge, Victor could feel the man's fingers brushing the back of his windbreaker. Before he could think of his next move, Renard brought him to the hard pavement. Victor rolled in pain. When he opened his eyes, the stranger was upon him.

"I'm not playing around anymore!" Renard growled as he hit Victor violently with his fist.

The bartender let out a cry as he felt the man lift him to his feet and violently push him to the side of the bridge.

"For the last time, asshole," Renard hissed. "Where is it?!"

Victor squirmed to run but couldn't move. He felt his spine crack as Renard pushed him harder against the cool metal rail.

"Wait!" Victor exclaimed as he tried to steady himself and scrambled for something to grab.

But, it was too late. His center of gravity shifted over the rail. Renard tried to change his grip, and the bartender's jacket slipped through his fingers. Suddenly Victor fell free of Renard's hold. Before the bartender realized what was happening, he was falling toward water.

Chapter XIV.

The air in the bar was cold. Still positioned between the curtain and the group, Renard stood motionless as all eyes came to rest upon him.

"You killed Victor?!" Trudel shouted.

Renard said nothing.

"Trudel, dear," Fleuse sighed sympathetically while moving toward her.

Trudel let out a primal shriek and reached for her highball glass. She hurled it in Renard's direction, not caring that there was still a finger of whiskey left inside. Peukington's man instantly ducked for cover as the item sped by his head and shattered on the wall behind him.

"Hey!" I yelled instinctively. Janie shielded her head, although she was nowhere near the shattered glass.

Pistache dove under a table as Trudel stood in a rage. She also threw an ashtray toward Renard, then an empty wine glass, but he continued to dance out of the way. A container full of cocktail napkins and straws, another two glasses, and a beer bottle sped his way.

"We were in love!" Trudel spat. "You took him away from me!"

"Trudel, dear …" Fleuse tried, approaching her cautiously. She jumped when he put his hand on her shoulder.

"Get off me!" she yelled through tears. She stormed toward a table and lifted a chair above her head.

"Darling, no!" Fleuse yelled, diving out of the way.

"I'm not your darling!" she exclaimed as she pitched the chair at Renard. Huffing, she picked up another one. I was impressed with her strength.

Renard dodged projectile after projectile. "Would you just listen?!" he screamed more than once.

After a few chairs, the opera singer stooped to pick up the safe. She hoisted it into her arms, but unsurprisingly couldn't throw it like she had a chair. She mustered a deep breath and heaved it toward the man, but couldn't keep her balance. Unable to let it go properly, she came crashing down on a tabletop with the safe. She lay sobbing among the splintered pieces of the shattered table when Janie and Fleuse arrived at her side.

"Are you okay?" Janie asked as she clasped Trudel's hand. "Let's get you up."

With Fleuse's help, Janie was able to get her to her feet.

"Let's find somewhere to sit you down," Fleuse suggested.

"Good luck," Pistache said, still hiding under a table. "She just destroyed half the chairs in here."

"Listen," Renard tried to explain. "I didn't intend to or even want to kill Victor Laquer!"

"Horseshit!" Trudel spat through the tears.

"Think about it!" Peukington's man continued. "Why would I want to get rid of my best lead?!"

Pistache leapt from hiding. "So she throws some bar stuff at you, are you going to kill her next?!"

"Of course not," Renard angrily shouted.

"Well, don't act so surprised that I've posed the question. It is obvious that the game has changed now."

"How has the game changed?" Renard asked. "You still stole something and I need it back!"

"Yes, before it was about this damned coin. Now it is about murder!" Pistache yelled. "Is anyone getting out of this bar alive unless we produce the coin?

And then, what will happen? You might kill us anyway!"

Janie sat down with Trudel. Although they spent time beating each other up in the card game, I saw Janie pat the opera singer's hand.

Trying to diffuse the situation, I slowly came out from behind the bar.

"I'm not trying to leave right now," I cautiously explained. "Let's all try to calm down. Everyone grab a chair, sit at a table, and let's just talk about this like adults."

No one moved.

"Well, I'll tell you what," Pistache ranted on, staring at Renard. "I sure don't plan on letting this go on any longer. I'm taking off."

"Jacques," Renard spat. "We've been over this. You know I can't let you walk out of here right now."

"Who says that you can stop me?" Pistache hissed back.

"Jacques," Fleuse muttered quickly.

"What?!" Pistache said out of the corner of his mouth.

"Jacques," Fleuse said again.

"Dammit, Fleuse! What?!" Pistache yelled, snapping his head toward the clockmaker.

"I don't think you want to go."

"Why the hell not?!"

"Well look," Fleuse said with a motion toward the splintered table.

The safe sat exactly where Trudel fell with it. It was resting on its backside, and I had to turn my head to see the dial. To all of our astonishment, the safe's door had finally popped slightly open.

"I don't believe it," Pistache said quietly.

"I did it," Trudel whispered proudly with tears still on her face.

Pistache rolled his eyes at the woman.

"Well for God's sake," Janie said. "Someone just look inside the damned thing."

Renard approached the safe. He knelt beside it and slowly peered inside. "Wow."

"What's in it?" Fleuse asked.

"Uh …" Renard said with a chuckle. "This might not be easy. Let's get it up."

Fleuse stood to help, but Renard quickly continued, "No, stay where you are. I need the American to give me a hand."

All eyes on the room landed on me just in time to witness my surprise. "Me?"

Renard began to position himself over the safe to lift it. "Yes you. I just need help moving this. Let's get it up to the bar, then we can sort through the contents."

"Well, what's inside?" I asked again, joining Peukington's man.

"Yeah, is the coin there?" Janie echoed.

"I don't know," Renard answered. "Have a look." He tilted the safe in my direction so I could best see through the open door. Light from the overheads splashed across the inside of the safe. I almost gasped when I saw not one, but many glistening coins of all sizes and metals. Each one was different.

I slowly knelt as I registered the scene. "Treasure," I whispered in awe.

"It's got to be Victor's collection," Pistache muttered.

"His collection is bigger than that," Fleuse said.

"I thought he'd sold most of it off," Trudel answered.

"Did he ever mention any part of the collection here?" Fleuse asked her.

"I don't think so," she said.

"It would make sense that he didn't store it all in one place," Renard muttered.

"I guess," I said.

"C'mon, help me move this thing," Renard urged.

I stooped across from him, and we lifted the safe. The door swung freely as we moved it to the bar top. The others migrated in our direction. We carefully placed the safe on the bar. I heard fabric ripping as we turned the object toward Renard and the others.

"Oh, honey," Janie gasped lightly, almost smiling. "Your shirt."

My good sleeve had momentarily been caught on the door, and a tear nearly separated the cuff from the rest of the sleeve. "Damn," I uttered.

"Were you still planning on wearing that shirt after this evening?" Pistache asked.

Janie chuckled. "It's seen better nights."

I sighed. The shirt was pretty much already ruined, but it was still my favorite blue plaid. I rolled the cuff to keep it from catching on something else.

Renard went to work. Opening the door as widely as possible, he began removing coin after coin. He did so two or three at a time, giving each handful a quick glance before grunting and setting them aside. For the moment, it looked as though he no longer cared about anyone leaving through the curtain. That is, it seemed that way until Pistache took a step in that direction.

"Just a moment, Monsieur Pistache," Renard motioned in his direction without looking up.

"Damn it," Pistache said. "Make me a drink, American."

"You name it," I answered.

"Just whiskey."

"What's that?" Fleuse asked as he casually pointed at something Renard had removed from the safe without much thought.

"Looks like a napkin or something," Renard grunted as he examined another handful of coin.

Fleuse approached and picked up what indeed was a cocktail napkin. Casting a critical eye over the top of his glasses, he held it delicately.

"Why was there a cocktail napkin in there?" Janie asked.

"I don't know," Fleuse replied. "There might be something written on it." He carefully unfolded the thin paper until it was only one ply. Low and behold, there was a drawing on it, lightly traced in pencil or faded pen.

"What is it?" Trudel asked.

"It looks like a layout of this room," Fleuse said as he continued his examination.

"Maybe it's a map, like, a treasure map," I said half-jokingly.

"Maybe," said Fleuse. "There are people's names placed all around the room."

"Whose names?" Renard asked.

"Well, just people," Fleuse continued. "Look here's Trudel."

"Am I on there?" Pistache asked.

"No, but I am," Fleuse mentioned. His name was next to Trudel's at the bar area.

"Who are the rest of these people?" Renard asked.

"Actually, I don't know," Fleuse answered as his finger traced lines from name to name, placed at tables around all corners of the room. "Susan, Lillian …"

"Hussies," Trudel spat quietly.

"This is where we usually sit though," he added.

I leaned in for a closer look. "I love how he's drawn a star where he stands. Kind of a 'you are here' indication like a map at the mall," I observed.

"Yeah, that's funny," Janie said.

"Hmm," Fleuse laughed a little. "Yes."

"What did Victor mean by this seating chart?" Renard asked.

"Well, let's be fair here. Are we assuming Victor even drew the map?" I said. "Is there a name on it? Any indication that it was his?"

"Well, no," Fleuse answered.

"Why not put his own name behind the bar?" Janie asked.

"He didn't need to know his own name," Pistache said with contemptuous tone.

"Well, he didn't need to know Trudel's or Fleuse's either," I pointed out. "But they're there."

Renard had resumed the coin inventory.

"He's just jealous that I'm on the map and he's not," Trudel stated.

"I am not," Pistache said.

"So maybe this was a seating chart for some kind of event?" I offered.

"There aren't events in here," Trudel said.

"Surely, hotel guests must have occasions. Maybe Victor was supposed to be planning something."

"This place is pretty slow usually," she said.

"Yeah," Fleuse added. "Just doesn't seem right."

"It's not here," Renard said, rejoining the conversation. He sat with the emptied safe in front of him. There was a significant amount of currency piled on the bar in front of him. I didn't recognize any of the coins as euros, or even francs.

"Damn it," Pistache whispered with an eye roll and a swig of his newest libation.

"Are you sure?" Trudel asked.

"Positive," Renard said.

"If your boss kept it on his person at all times," I began, "then how would you know exactly what it looked like? There are a lot of coins there."

"Well, he had the item pretty well documented," Renard stated. "Plus, a lot of these aren't even French. Truly, this has to be part of Victor's collection. There is no way that this is bar money or anything."

"Yeah, I didn't think it was," I said.

"Well," Renard said as he gently shrugged. "I guess I'll take a drink too."

*   *   *

Bees' hearts beat faster when there's honey in the hive. I read one of Janie's cocktail-napkin poems that she'd left on the bar. She'd completed several one-liners as she scribbled throughout the night. I don't know how she'd remained so relaxed.

I nervously cleaned glassware. For a party of five people, it seemed as though we had gone through enough pints and highballs for an entire dining room. Then again, we broke as many as we didn't.

It was starting to feel late. Janie and I had missed our regular dinner hour, but in the excitement of the evening we'd failed to notice until now. We'd also failed to address the imminent danger of the situation.

"Psst, honey!" I whispered as I dried a glass. Janie walked over, as the rest of the room apparently didn't notice.

"Hey baby," she answered.

"So, are we going to ignore the fact that this guy killed someone?" I motioned toward Renard. "Shouldn't we be trying a little harder to get the hell out of here?"

Janie subtly looked in his direction. Renard was staring at his half-drunk glass.

"I don't know. I don't think that he'll actually hurt us."

"Maybe," I said. "He does seem pretty reasonable, but he just admitted that he killed someone."

"Yeah, I get that. But do you really want to test him and just try to walk out of here?"

"Not really," I guessed.

"Plus, think about this: He hasn't been at all close to violent tonight. Nor has he even said that he has a weapon on him."

"I guess you're right," I sighed. "But still, this is serious. I need to keep you safe." I puffed my chest a little.

"Please. Exhale, baby. You'd have more credibility if your shirt wasn't in four pieces."

I did look ridiculous. She was right.

"Let me ask you this," she continued. "There's a good chance that this coin of theirs isn't anywhere in here."

"Yeah, I've thought of that."

"So don't you want to know where it has ended up?"

"Truthfully, I'm a little more concerned about getting out of here right now," I answered.

"No, I know. But think about it for a second. When we look back on this later, won't it be annoying to not know?"

"I guess."

"I mean," she insisted, "we're going to wind up telling people about tonight. It's an incredible thing to happen to us. Won't it be such a shame if we have an undefined ending?"

I thought about it seriously as I washed a glass. "Not knowing might make it better, actually," I answered, shrugging.

"I suppose."

I switched gears, and nodded at the coins. "So, how do they look?"

"They're cool," she answered, looking down at the bar top. Janie and Fleuse had meticulously laid out each coin from the safe. Even an inch apart, they took up a large expanse of bar-top real estate. Trudel watched them organize over her shoulder, and all three occasionally made comments about which ones they liked. Most were in foreign languages and bore the faces of unfamiliar royalty. Pistache sat alone at a table out on the floor.

While whispering with Janie, I'd noticed Renard's spirit had deflated. He wasn't guarding the curtain with any fervor, but he was seated at the end of the bar closest to it. His drink sat in front of him. It was a lonely look, as if he'd been through a breakup. I was beginning to feel badly for him. He noticed me looking at him.

"So, your girl says you're a writer," he said.

"A journalist, yes."

"I imagine this is plenty of fodder for you."

"Well, I write about news and events mostly. I'm not sure how I'd approach this experience."

He lightly shrugged. "Listen, write whatever you want. Just don't mention Monsieur Peukington. I'm serious about that."

"Of course." I was unwilling to mess with a guy who threw someone off a bridge.

"Good. Did you know that you're bleeding?" he asked with a nod toward my hand.

I looked down. It wasn't much, and I hadn't felt it. Really not more than a scratch across the top of one of my fingers, it had been bleeding slowly. It had to have happened during the safe moving.

"Huh, I didn't see that," I automatically answered. Instinctively, I wiped it on the front of my shirt.

Janie looked up. "Honey, give me a break. You have soap, a sink, and towels back there. How old are you?"

"That's true," I admitted. "Who knows how nasty these towels are, though?"

I washed my hand. Since things had finally calmed down in the bar, for the first time it occurred to me that I might want to let the concierge know that we had found the safe.

"So, listen," I said to Renard. "I know that you haven't really found what you're looking for, and I am beginning to feel as though it might not be in here."

He made a face and took a drink.

I continued, "So, my wife and I haven't eaten yet, and we were headed out to dinner when we came in here this evening."

"We're way beyond dinner now, honey," Janie said. I had no idea why she would say something that might keep us from getting out of there.

"Well, cafés are still open," I said hopefully.

"Very few. Kitchens won't be anywhere," Fleuse muttered as he tilted a coin in his hand toward the light.

"Well, the point is," I continued for Renard, "that it seems like things here have kind of reached … an impasse."

"The coin is in here. I'm sure of it," he said with another drink.

"I know that you keep saying that, but are you sure that we need to be here while you find it?"

He finished the drink and set the glass down in front of him. "Look. You two have been very friendly. I like you both, and you've been helpful. Do I think that you are concealing the coin? No. Can I be absolutely sure that you are not? Also no."

"We don't have it!" Janie protested.

"Yeah, if I had it," I said, "I would just give it to you."

"Would you really?" Pistache asked as he stood. "Yes."

"Think about it though," the pickpocket went on as he approached the bar. "It's valuable."

"Yes, I know," I said.

"I don't know you, but my guess is that you have probably never held anything that valuable before."

"True," I said. "But if this thing really belongs to some businessman, then I wouldn't keep it."

"Stop calling him that!" Pistache exclaimed and retreated back to his table.

I looked to Renard who wasn't saying anything.

"Why not?" I asked. "This Peukington guy? I thought that's what he was."

"Well, he is a businessman," Renard said while tapping the edge of the empty glass. "But ..."

"He's a very dangerous businessman," Pistache yelled out.

"What do you mean, dangerous?" I asked as I refilled Renard's drink.

"Think about it," Trudel hissed as she locked eyes on Renard. "Businessmen don't kill people."

There was a momentary silence.

"He does business, though," Renard refuted.

"Do you get it yet?!" Pistache yelled toward me. "He is a bad guy! The cops look for ways to get him."

"For what?" I asked.

"Not all his business is legal," Renard said simply.

"Not all his business is legal?" Pistache huffed. "Heh, I'll say. He ordered you to kill Victor."

"That is not exactly true," Renard stated. "I really wasn't supposed to kill him."

"No one is saying it, but I will," Fleuse chimed in as he placed a coin he held back on the counter. He looked at me. "Monsieur Peukington is a gangster."

"Do you get it now?" Pistache again stood. "This guy, Renard obviously works for him. He's kind of a henchman. He's not a trained killer or anything, but he's muscle. You are not targets of his, but if you try to go anywhere he'll probably make sure that you don't have the coin. And he won't care if you're conscious or not while he checks."

"He seems to like you guys, though," Fleuse added positively. "Maybe he wouldn't kill you like he did Victor."

I looked to Renard, who confirmed the accusation without saying anything. I sighed and reached for a bottle of whiskey. Removing the pour top, I took a swig straight from the bottle. Exasperated by the situation, I was hoping that the booze would help me feel numb to it. My eyes immediately watered from the quick swallow. Pistache huffed in amusement.

I looked in Janie's direction, expecting to see a horrified and scared spouse. If anything though, she was distracted. I worried that the sudden rush of booze had skewed my perception, but she wasn't even looking back. I saw her staring at the curtain.

"Who is that?" she said softly. All heads turned toward the entrance, and there was an audible wave of gasps that rushed over the room.

I looked toward the curtain as well and saw a thin, old face peering back at us through shadows beyond the opening in the drape. I thought I was imagining it all before I blinked a few times and the apparition did not dissipate.

The visage barely reacted to being noticed by the group in the bar. Reduced to a gasp, I heard the one word Trudel could muster.

"Victor!"

Chapter XV.

The trip from the bridge to the water was longer than Victor Laquer expected. It didn't look like much from a distance. He'd never leapt from anything higher than a diving board in his youth, so the concept of really falling was altogether foreign.

He heard the smack as he hit. Icy water burned his skin numb. His heart punched the inside of his chest. He kicked. There was no bottom. The current immediately pushed him.

Dizzied by the fall and disoriented, Victor somehow found a way to find the surface, even if only for a moment. He craned his neck. Keeping his head above water was much harder than he would have thought. He stretched to get a glimpse of the banks between interrupted gasps for air. No one was there to notice.

Victor's moments were passing quickly, and it wasn't long before he realized that he was in trouble. He kicked off his loafers. Muscles instantly ached. He struggled to stay afloat. Panic. Sucking air. For the first time in his life, Victor thought that he was going to die.

He couldn't have been in the water for more than half a minute. The bartender's perception of time was skewed. He knew it was only a second or two before his head would sink below the water's surface. However, those two seconds of swimming saved him. It was just enough time to notice a rope among the waves.

Victor didn't know where it had come from, but it lay on the surface of the water, floating in a mess of turns and loops. He didn't know why he even reached for it, but he did. It provided little comfort. The rope did not have nearly the buoyancy it needed to keep him from slipping under. But, still he held it in his hand.

The notion of holding on to this rope felt futile quickly. For all he knew, it was river trash thrown from one of the many quiet houseboats and barges that lined the river's edge. Suddenly, something pulled the rope. The line sped through his hand. He tightened his grip and was on the move.

He wasn't going anywhere quickly, but it was suddenly easier to keep his head above water. He rubbed the river from his eyes and was happy to see someone actively pulling him toward a houseboat. With the deck of the long, flat boat towering above him, Victor was happy to realize that there was a ladder along the vessel's side.

Upon grabbing it, he felt his arms give out. Victor spent so much energy trying to stay alive in the river, that he was unsure now if he could even drag himself up to safety.

Still, he threw his hand at the next thin cold metal rung, and then again at the next. He felt a strong hand grip his collar, and suddenly the strain on his own muscles was lifted as he felt his shirt begin to pull him upward.

Victor was finally lying on the deck of the boat in a puddle of water. He inhaled air in giant gulps. The deck was hard and unforgiving. Gravity pulled him to it so ferociously that his face started to hurt.

"Are you okay?" a woman's voice asked.

Victor's eyes were open, but he hadn't thought yet to look upon the person who had saved him.

"Hey," she repeated. "Are you okay?"

"Yes," he mustered through labored breaths. "Thank you."

"What happened?"

He finally was able to focus on her. How she had been able to pull him from the water with such ease was a mystery. She was short. Her wiry black hair was tied in back, and her blue sweater was old and ratty. She stood next to an unfinished wooden chair, hovering over him. Her long skirt stopped just above her bare feet.

"I was thrown off the bridge," he blurted out.

"What?!" she asked with surprise.

"Well, I ..." He wasn't sure how to explain it. Victor was out of breath still just trying to talk.

"Come on," she urged. "Let's get you up."

Before Victor knew what was happening, she had him on his feet.

"You had better come inside, it's cold," she continued. It was still summer, but the nights had begun to cool considerably, and he shivered.

She walked him passed some weathered outdoor furniture on the boat's deck through a small doorway. Victor had to duck. Bathed in the soft yellow light, the bartender collapsed in a chair. A light hung from the ceiling, practically tapping him on the forehead. He felt his clothing being removed. It felt better.

"Take off your pants," the woman said. "My husband has a pair that will work. Or I can just get you a blanket."

Victor, still in shock, complied. "A blanket is fine," he muttered. "Thank you for the help. Who are you?"

"I'm Sarah," she said through the door as she hung his clothes over the railing outside. "You said that someone threw you off a bridge?"

"Well, yes," he replied simply as she returned to him. He wasn't sure how much he should explain.

Victor looked around. He sat in a room that clearly doubled as kitchen and dining area. The woman kept numerous houseplants in every corner on the space. There was barely room to walk. Pots and pans hung from the ceiling, and Victor was reminded of the bar. Sarah fit under them all, a remarkably small woman.

"Do you live here?" he asked.

"Yes. Let me make some coffee. You need to warm up."

"You live on a boat?" Victor asked.

"I do," she answered with a snicker. "I live on this boat."

For a moment, Victor considered retirement on a boat. Then, he remembered his current circumstances. The future of the coin was suddenly very much undetermined, and it seemed he had less claim to it than ever.

"So are you going to tell me who threw you off the bridge?"

Victor snapped out of his daydream. "I actually don't know him."

"So you were randomly thrown off a bridge? I hope that trend doesn't catch on."

"Not exactly. He did introduce himself first."

"I don't want to pry," Sarah said as she sat at the table with a cup of coffee for herself. "But, it seems like there is more to this story."

"Well, there is."

"I know we just met, but why do I get the feeling that you might have deserved to be thrown off the bridge?"

Victor chuckled. "Yes, maybe. Who knows?" he said as he took a sip. He was beginning to feel more like himself.

"What's your name?" Sarah asked.

"Victor."

"Good. Since you were thrown off a bridge and I saved you, a police officer might one day ask me about it. I want to at least tell them I asked," she said nonchalantly.

The bartender liked her. She made him feel comfortable.

"Victor Laquer," he said as he extended his hand, finally having fully caught his breath.

*   *   *

Victor emerged from the kitchen in the cool grey morning light. Sarah let him sleep on a trundle that pulled out from a bench along the side of the kitchen table. There had been barely room to move, but he'd been warm and comfortable. His muscles were so numb and tired from the river, it had been a solid sleep.

His hostess had left some of her husband's clothes for him to wear. They were slightly too big for him, but Victor didn't mind. When he emerged onto the deck of the houseboat, he saw Sarah seated at an outdoor table. He didn't know why she'd trusted him, but he felt a particular kindness toward her as well.

"Good morning," she said as she sipped coffee and turned the page on a newspaper. Her bony hand gripped the mug, stretching leather skin over her knuckles.

"Do you get the paper delivered on the river?" he asked, jokingly.

"Actually yes," she answered. "Someone comes along every morning."

Victor walked to the railing and looked up and down the quai. The boat had not moved from the night before. Many others like it were tied to the shore near Sarah's. He looked up the great stone walls that lined the river and saw backs of kiosks that lined the sidewalk above. Behind him, he viewed the distant opposite riverbank.

"Would you like a cup of coffee?" Sarah asked.

"Sure," he answered, looking at other houseboats. "Do you know the other people tied up along here?"

"I have met him," she said as she nodded to the houseboat directly in front of hers. "But, not many others. There's a pot of coffee right here. Empty mugs are inside. The cabinet above the wash basin."

"I wasn't sure if this was a regular neighborhood or anything," Victor thought aloud, ducking back inside briefly. "If everyone's houses come and go, I suppose not."

"Actually, that is not exactly the case," she called after him. "I have been tied here for years."

"Doesn't that defeat the purpose of having a moving house?"

"Well, my husband and I don't crave change the way some boat owners do."

"Interesting," Victor noted as he emerged.

"So Victor," Sarah began. "Now that you are rested and dry, I take it you won't be staying here today. I'll just need those clothes back before you go. I have yours drying on a line near the bow. They should be ready within an hour or so."

Victor nodded as he poured coffee. "Thank you."

"I don't think you came aboard with shoes," Sarah said, looking at the bartender's feet.

"Oh, right."

"I have an old pair of sandals that you can take if you need them."

"That's great, thank you. You have been very hospitable."

"Well, I have many visitors when my husband is away. Sometimes it's people we know, other times it's people in need."

"Seems dangerous," Victor said, sitting down across from her. An all-weather area rug felt cold and hard on his bare feet. "Doesn't your husband worry that someone will hurt you when he's gone?"

"Maybe," she smiled. "But I don't tell him half the time."

"Well, I'd be worried," he said.

"That's sweet of you. You have enough to be worried about for yourself though," she said. "You got thrown off a bridge."

"True."

"I'm sure that you're in good shape now. Surely the guy isn't still up there waiting for you," Sarah mused.

Victor sipped his coffee. "Well, I certainly hope not, but I can't be too sure about it."

"Oh yeah?"

Victor paused as he stared into the blackness of his mug.

"The thing is," Victor answered, "I did something wrong."

"I'm listening."

"Something illegal."

Sarah shifted in her chair.

"Oh don't worry," Victor continued. "The police aren't after me or anything. At this stage, it could really just be classified as a personal problem with someone."

"Am I in trouble for having you here?" Sarah asked, voicing her obvious concern.

"No," the bartender answered. "Still, I should be off."

"Well, hang on. Now I'm curious. Your clothes still need to dry anyway. So, out with it. What happened?"

With a sigh, Victor told her everything.

*   *   *

Victor stayed another night on the barge with Sarah. As he'd recounted the situation to her over coffee that morning, he'd somehow earned enough of her trust to gain the invitation.

The bartender had learned that Sarah herself was a fairly free-spirited person. Her husband was a business-minded man, who truly seemed to love her eccentricities, perhaps due to a lack of any himself.

"So you don't mind him being gone?" Victor asked as the two sat on the deck at night. The soft morning sky had been replaced with stars. Instead of coffee, a bottle of brandy sat on the table.

Wrapped in a blanket, Sarah answered, "I would of course rather have him here. But, I definitely don't mind that he has his business."

Victor nodded.

"So," she said. "What about Trudel? The woman you mentioned this morning?"

"What about her?" Victor grunted.

"Will you be running away with her?"

"I honestly hadn't planned for that really. It never occurred to me that she would even want to leave."

Sarah sat with her feet tucked beneath a blanket, gently swirling her brandy with the motion of her glass.

Pausing in thought, Victor added, "I actually didn't really think that we'd wind up together forever anyway."

"I gathered, based on what you said this morning about the time in the café with her."

Victor took a sip of brandy.

"May I weigh in here?" Sarah asked.

"Sure."

"I think you should leave alone. Head down to the Riviera like you wanted to."

"I can't. That guy Julian Renard probably has the coin by now. Who knows what's happened to Fleuse and Jacques? Or even Trudel, for that matter."

"Do you think he'd be able to find the coin?"

"I don't know."

"Well, you're going to have to come out of hiding sometime. What are you going to do?"

Victor shrugged.

Sarah continued, "If he has found the coin, this guy probably isn't going to be after you anymore."

"But if he hasn't found the coin, he'll probably throw me off another bridge," the bartender added with a soft laugh. They both drank.

"Do you mind if I give you a metaphor?"

"Not at all," Victor said.

"Well, my husband and I like to play chess. Sometimes, he thinks he has my king pinned down. To be honest, sometimes he really does because he is much better than I am at chess."

Victor snickered. He could never play games like that with Trudel. She'd take a loss too personally.

"But," Sarah continued. "He is so used to being better than me at chess, that he doesn't notice his own flaws. Sometimes, he thinks he has me pinned down, but it is really I who have the upper hand. As he kills off my players, he doesn't realize that I have positioned his own pawns where I need them."

"Clever."

"With his own piece on the offensive, his king is open. Do you see what I'm saying?"

"Somehow use other people to defend myself? I don't get it," Victor answered.

"I lead him to believe he is winning, then I use his own pawns against him. And that's when I win."

"So are you saying that I somehow have the upper hand here? That I can turn the tables?"

"Maybe you can. This stranger who was following you thinks you're dead."

"That's true."

"It helps that you haven't left this boat. Unless someone's been watching you here—and there's no reason to think that anyone has—then you are currently presumed dead or missing by everyone else."

"But I still won't be able to go get the coin without being seen."

"Maybe, maybe not."

"I suppose I could try to sneak in."

"You could. It's not a terrible idea. But consider this: Why not try to use Peukington's pawn against him?"

Victor sipped his brandy.

Sarah went on, "they think they're winning. If you were truly a bold player in this, I'd say it's time to turn the tables."

Chapter XVI.

"Where the hell have you been?!" Trudel shouted as she leapt to her feet and charged at the bartender.

"Victor!" Fleuse shouted as Trudel sped by.

Renard stared at the man. Victor took a step backward in the doorway as Trudel approached. I had trouble telling if she would embrace or strike him.

"Where have you been!?" she screamed again. "You weren't dead?!" She slapped away at the curtain as if she was angry with the folds, but I knew Victor was in there somewhere. Fleuse finally caught up with her and pulled her back, and Victor finally entered the room.

"Take it easy, Trudie!" he said as he recovered from the mini-attack. He took a look around the room. "Well everyone is here, even Julian Renard."

"How did you ..." Renard mustered.

Victor didn't let him finish. He swung just once, hard and fast. His fist connected with Renard's chin. It wasn't enough to put him on the floor, but it was a solid warning shot anyway. Renard rubbed his face. His expression indicated that he got the point.

"That's for throwing me off a bridge, asshole," Victor grunted.

"Where have you been?" Fleuse asked.

"You guys opened my safe?!" Victor exclaimed as he noticed all the currency spread across the bar. "How did you get into it?" He asked as he pulled a hand-rolled cigarette out of his pocket.

Renard huffed, "Like it did us any good, anyway."

"I am the one who actually got it open," Trudel momentarily beamed with spite. "I hope you hate that, you bastard. We touched every single coin!"

"Shut up, Trudie," Victor mumbled with cigarette in his mouth. He was fishing in his pocket for a matchbook.

"Don't change the subject!" she yelled. "I need to know everything! Where the hell have you been!?"

Victor was too busy taking inventory of all his coins. "None seem to be missing ..." The bartender struck a match and lit the cigarette as he perused his collection, seemingly eyeing every detail.

"Victor!"

"Trudel," Victor said, sounding exhausted. "I will tell you everything if you just relax for a second. There really isn't too much of a big deal, here. This bastard here throws me off a bridge, I swim around, a woman pulls me on to her boat ..."

"A woman?! I knew it!"

Victor ignored her and looked directly at me. "Who is this?" He asked the room.

"Hi, I'm Peter," I said haplessly. "This is my wife, Janie. We are on vacation, and the concierge has allowed us to come in for a drink or two."

"It looks as though it's been more than a drink or two," Victor answered as he looked around. He was right. The state of things made it seem as though a raging party were taking place. I guess it was.

Victor continued, "And, what has happened to you?"

"What do you mean what has happened to me?" I answered.

"Surely your shirt didn't look like that when you walked in here."

I had almost forgotten that my favorite blue plaid barely had any structure anymore. Between the rips and the burns, I must have looked as though I had just escaped a shipwreck.

"Oh, right. Yeah, it's in bad shape."

"There's an extra one of mine behind the bar, I think. You can wear it if you want," Victor offered offhandedly. It didn't occur to me to put on the old shirt behind the bar.

"Thanks," I said as I grabbed the flannel. The new shirt was a little dusty, but it was comfortable, warm, and dry.

"Do you want to take over back here?" I asked.

"No. I'm sure that you're doing fine. Besides, my job here is probably gone since I've been missing."

"Actually," I mused as I buttoned the old black-checkered shirt, "they obviously don't have a replacement for you yet."

If he heard me, he didn't care. "So ..." Victor said, switching gears. "Who has the coin?"

"It's not in here," Fleuse sighed. "We've checked everywhere."

"I will not let you ignore me," Trudel spat. "I don't care if you never want to see me again, but I am owed an explanation!"

"Who said that I never wanted to see you again?"

"Well you leave for a few weeks, so I have begun to get the idea!"

Victor shrugged. "So I was not around for a little while, who cares!? It's not like we are married or anything!"

"Don't you think she deserved to know where you were?" Fleuse interjected.

"You couldn't keep her warm for me, Newman?" Victor jabbed with a smile. Fleuse grimaced. Trudel almost cried.

"You bastard. I hate you," she choked off.

"Victor," Renard interrupted. "Welcome back. You can sort out all your issues with this woman later. For now, maybe you can clear something up for us, because this evening is becoming more than frustrating." Renard slowed his speech pattern and spoke deliberately. "Give me the Peukington coin, and we can call it a night. Right now."

"Argh!" Pistache finally piped up. "It's obviously not here! This is a dead end, Renard."

"No, it's here," Victor cut-in. "Unless someone smuggled it out of here this evening."

"No one has left," Renard grunted.

"Well, someone got it then," Victor said.

"What do you mean, someone got it?" Janie asked, unable to restrain her curiosity.

"Well, it was hidden in here, and it's not there now," Victor said.

"Was it in the safe?" I asked.

"Obviously not," Victor grunted. "You've gone through my private things with such care. Surely you would have noticed had it been there."

"What was with that napkin?" Janie asked. I knew that she was dying for some answers.

"Well, that's it. It was a reminder of my hiding spots among other things. It didn't lead you to the coin?"

"We found your letter under the bar," Trudel interrupted. She obviously didn't care about the coin. "What was that shit?"

"What were the names on the napkin?" Pistache wondered aloud as well.

"Okay Trudie. First of all, you can't threaten to kill me and not expect me to worry a little. I'd had a few drinks and hid that envelope."

"I never said I'd kill you!" she hissed with a flourish of her hand.

"You did too!"

"When?!" she shouted.

"That night here. After one of your shows," Victor raised his voice.

"Excuse me," Pistache interrupted. "Does this have anything to do with anything?"

"No," Victor shot him a look. "She is just crazy, and I was drunk."

Trudel ignored the comment and shouted at Victor, "Well, I didn't mean it. I love you. I could never hurt you!"

"I think you said that you'd stab my eyeballs with toothpicks," he answered. "Anyway, I'm really not that worried about it."

The blood behind Trudel's face warmed ten degrees in an instant as she struggled to conjure up a response.

"I hate you so much," she again specified.

"What about the names?" Janie repeated Pistache's question.

"Well, I do that pretty often, I'm sure you understand," Victor said with a glance in my direction. "I'm working for tips back there, so I'm trying to remember everyone's name in the place. Sometimes there just are too many folks to get right off the top of my head. I just wound up using that particular napkin for my hiding places as well."

"Focus, Laquer," Renard said. "Just cough up the coin. I'm running out of patience."

"Well, it was right there!" Victor exclaimed with a motion toward me.

Renard immediately snapped his head as his eyes frantically scoured the bar area. "Where exactly?"

"Well, it's no mystery! Fleuse, Jacques, and Trudie all know where it is. The Americans probably even saw it back there."

"What? Where?!" Renard asked.

"The star on the map you found. I saved that napkin for a reason."

"We thought the star was you," Janie interjected.

"Why would I need to know where I was?" Victor answered.

"That's what I tried to tell them!" Pistache exclaimed.

"It's like at the mall," I said.

"What?" the former bartender answered. "The star was the coin, not me."

No one else in the room seemed to react extraordinarily to the situation, and Janie and I suddenly knew that we had been on the outside of something the entire time. Did the others really know where the coin had been all along?

"I don't see it!" Renard continued as he moved to the edge of the bar.

"Well, of course you don't. It's not there now. Someone grabbed it," Victor snapped.

"Where are we looking?" I asked.

"The clock, obviously," Victor motioned directly behind me. "That's where it's been for the last few weeks at least, right where Fleuse inlaid it."

I wheeled around to the clock. I hadn't originally noticed, but there was a small space on the ornate face of the timepiece that was missing decoration. The inlay was so detailed that I hadn't seen the empty slot at first.

"He built it into the face of a clock," Janie explained to herself with a degree of satisfaction. "Hid it in plain sight."

"Where is it now?" Renard barked as he addressed the room.

"Someone has it," Victor said casually. "I've kept an eye on this place."

"How could you have kept an eye on this place if you were with another woman?" Trudel asked.

"Dammit! Are you serious?" Victor snapped. "Just take it easy."

"No, Victor!" Trudel yelled as she stood tall. "The time has come for us to break up!"

"You think?" he answered with a snide tone.

"Too long, have I waited for you. I assumed you were dead. Now, you waltz in here, so rude to me. I will not have it."

"Okay," Victor said with a shrug. He began to pickup each coin on the bar one by one and created small stacks.

"And now," Trudel continued in a rage. "I have found that you spent the last few weeks with another woman. Well, that's the last straw for me."

Without looking up from organizing his currency, he answered, "Well, I wasn't involved with her, but I suppose it doesn't matter."

"How can you be so cold to her?" Fleuse asked, now also standing.

Victor rolled his eyes still without turning around. "Ah Fleuse, still trying to be her knight in shining armor? Typical."

"She deserves better, Victor. And frankly, so do I."

Now, Pistache was standing as well. Sensing a changing tide in the room, Victor turned around.

"Why did you hide from us?" Pistache asked.

"Seriously, my friends. Take it easy," Victor said.

"Why not find us?" Pistache asked.

"You very well know that I couldn't let Renard here see us together. I wanted him to continue thinking I was dead."

"You could have snuck into my shop," Fleuse offered.

"Please. He's been watching your shop. I never felt as though there was ever going to be a safe time to get either of you alone."

"You could have at least found me," Trudel added with tears in her eyes. "I still don't believe he was ever following me."

"He was," Victor answered. "Besides, what was I going to say? It was pretty much over between us anyway."

Trudel's eyes widened with hurt. "Well at least you could have told me that! Coward!"

"I've had it!" Fleuse suddenly erupted. I didn't think he could yell like that. "You've got a great girl here, Victor. I've watched you squander your relationship and take her for granted for far too long!"

"You can have her," Victor snapped. "There. Are you finally happy?!"

"That's it." Fleuse said in disgust. He immediately turned toward the curtain. "The coin isn't even in here, and we've all put up with a lot tonight. I'm going to do what I should have done hours ago."

"Cough up the coin?" Victor asked, smiling.

"I'm leaving," the clockmaker announced defiantly.

Victor stepped in front of him. "And where do you think you're going?"

Renard looked on with marked interest.

"Anywhere. This place is a dead end."

"I'll let you walk out that door if you prove somehow that you don't have the coin," Victor said.

"Let me?!" Fleuse yelled. "Victor, we're on the same side!"

"Listen," the bartender went on. "This guy threw me off a bridge. We're beyond just hiding something."

"I don't know where it is!" Fleuse yelled.

"Still," the bartender answered. "It's time to put this whole thing to rest, and no one leaves."

"And how do you suggest I prove that I don't have the coin? Are you going to search me or something?! Or do you want me to just stand naked in front of you?!" Fleuse was livid.

"Impressive display, Fleuse," Pistache remarked snidely.

"Well," Victor answered. "It would be great if you simply produced the coin, or told me who had it."

"For the last time! I have no idea!"

Fleuse moved around the bartender and began his departure. Victor didn't even react. Expecting resistance from Renard, I immediately glanced to the man, whose placement near the curtain was unchanged. Only this time, he didn't move. He didn't even raise his head to break his stare at the carpet in front of him.

Fleuse stopped in his tracks and gasped. A tall man stood in the doorway, expressionless. I had never seen him before. Fleuse's entire demeanor changed instantly. He had been furious only a moment before, but the clockmaker was immediately tamed.

"Are you …?" Fleuse barely managed. Immediately, he blindly thrust his hand out behind him to feel for the nearest chair. When he found it, he grasped it and fell into the seat.

"And you are?" Trudel snapped.

The man's icy gaze surveyed the room.

"My name is Lavaar Peukington."

Chapter XVII.

Julian Renard sprinted through the narrow alley in the restaurant's kitchen. Men in white jackets and hats stared at him as he passed, frozen in their duties. They'd also heard the gunshots from the back room, but didn't dare rush through the door at the rear of the space.

Renard thrust the door open. A single light bulb swung lazily over a card table in the otherwise blackened room. A man in a suit lay face down, slumped over on the card table. Blood pooled slowly around him, staining the playing cards beneath him. Lavaar Peukington stood across the table from Renard, wiping a revolver with his bright white pocket square.

"What took you so long?"

"What took me so long?" Renard answered. "I was at a table right there, just like you said. How could I have possibly been any faster?"

"Aren't you going to start cleaning this up?" Peukington asked, nodding at the body. Blood had begun dripping over the side of the table on to the floor.

Renard wheeled around and looked back at the cooks, all of whom still stood and stared. Looking back toward Peukington, he finally managed, "but sir. They have seen everything."

"Don't worry. They won't say anything," the businessman said, eyeing the kitchen staff. The cooks immediately went right back to their work. "You should be concerned with other matters at this moment."

"Of course sir. What happened here?" Renard asked, shutting the door behind him.

Peukington tucked the revolver under his jacket and delicately removed his drink from the table.

"He was stealing from me."

"What did he take?" Renard gingerly lifted the dead man's wrist to confirm his condition.

"Actually, nothing yet," Peukington answered, taking a sip. "We've been trying to get a deal done for some time, but I discovered that he was being dishonest."

"I see. You should probably leave, sir," Renard suggested. "If anyone else heard those shots, we won't want to have you found here."

"I think I'll be okay," the businessman replied. He owned the entire building, and all the tenants knew Monsieur Peukington's nature.

Renard looked around the dark edges of the room. "Is there another light in here? This would be easier if it wasn't so dark."

Ignoring the question, Peukington again sipped from his drink. "Let me ask you. Do you remember anyone funny at the gala over the weekend?"

Renard thought back.

"I'm not sure what you mean?"

"Anyone out of place?" Peukington clarified.

"Not particularly. Why?" Renard circled the body, wondering how best to lift the man. Thinking twice about becoming covered in blood, he removed his jacket.

"My coin is gone."

"Your Napoleon coin?" Renard asked without looking up from his task.

"My family's coin," Peukington stated coolly, removing a cigarette from his jacket pocket.

"Right. You think you lost it at the party?"

"I don't think I lost it at all. I think it was stolen." Peukington lit his cigarette.

"Don't you carry it on you at all times?" Renard asked, searching from something in the room in which to wrap the body.

"Yes. I think it was taken right out of my pocket."

"Are you sure that you just didn't leave it in another jacket or something?"

Peukington shot him a look of complete frustration and leaned toward him. His eyes sparkled as he hissed, "Do you think I'm the kind of person that would make a fuss over something if I made mistakes like that?"

"Right."

"No, it was in my coat pocket when I went downstairs," Peukington continued. "I'm sure of it."

"So you were pickpocketed? Is that what you are saying?"

"That's what I'm saying. What are you doing?"

"I'm looking for some trash bags to wrap up this guy."

"I have an area rug in an office upstairs that I hate."

"Okay, I'll run up. I'll worry about the blood after I get him out of here."

"Plan for a long night. As usual, this place has to be completely scrubbed down," Peukington answered. "There can't be a single drop left in here. I am using this room to play mahjong tomorrow."

Renard thought carefully, thinking back to the coin before leaving the room. "So you're sure that you never took your coat off?"

Peukington drew on his cigarette. "Here's the bottom line: I want you to get it back for me."

"Okay," he said, gently pulling the dead man's head up long enough to see the anguished expression on his face. Renard didn't react. "There were quite a few people at that party. Do you have a lead on who it may have been?"

"I did go through the security footage, and I have a hunch when it happened. The man who did it was a crasher. I don't know his name because he wasn't invited, and he claimed to have met me previously. I doubt that, though. It appears that you may have spoken with him directly at the gala as well."

Renard thought back. He couldn't conceive of who it could have been. "Interesting," he mustered.

"I'll make sure you have access to the footage from the evening. It should give you a better idea of who to target."

Renard nodded along.

Peukington paused before taking a sip of his drink. "I'll make sure you are provided with all the documentation I have about the coin as well. I have several enlarged pictures of it for insurance reasons."

"Why not just claim the loss?" Renard asked.

"It's far more important to me than money. It is more valuable than money. It has been in my family for generations."

"I know," Renard answered.

"Excellent, now regarding your fee. As you know, I'm a fair man. You will be rewarded for your successful efforts. I'm willing to pay you eighty thousand euros for the coin."

Renard almost choked and placed his hand on the table to steady himself. Immediately feeling blood, he recoiled and noticed his handprint in the mess. Monsieur Peukington rolled his eyes.

"Thank you, sir," Renard stammered.

"Of course," Peukington said, smiling.

Now Renard wanted the coin more than anything. He reached to straighten his tie and accidentally wiped blood on the knot. Again, Peukington scoffed at his carelessness.

"Try to keep it together, Renard."

"Yes sir, of course. Sorry about that."

"Just get this taken care of. And tell the bartender to get me a fresh one of these on your way upstairs," Peukington remarked, shaking the ice in his glass.

"Of course. One last thing. What should I do with the person who has your coin when I find them?"

"I honestly don't care what happens to the person who took it. Rest assured, I'll kill him myself if I ever find him at one of my parties again."

Chapter XVIII.

"Do you have it?" Peukington grunted at Renard.

"Not yet," Renard answered with a sigh.

"You're Lavaar Peukington?!" Fleuse stammered. Apparently, everyone except Janie and I regarded this man as a little bit of a celebrity.

"Where is it?" Peukington asked simply. He was skipping all formal introductions.

"Hey, I recognize you!" I interjected. "You're the bust!"

The man looked at Renard. Neither spoke.

"Right here," I continued, pointing at the dignified man in bronze behind the bar. "This is you."

Peukington rolled his eyes.

Renard spoke for him. "That's Napoleon, idiot."

"Oh." There was a resemblance, though.

"I have followed these people relentlessly, sir," Renard answered Peukington's question. "I don't believe any of them actually have it right now."

"But someone must know where it is," Peukington eyed everyone suspiciously as he spoke.

"I don't disagree with that," Renard answered. "After my altercation with the old man Laquer, I actually think that it's somewhere here in this room."

"You mean when you threw him off a bridge and left him for dead?!" Trudel exclaimed.

Peukington gritted his teeth and subtly rolled his eyes.

Renard ignored Trudel. "The way that everyone flocked in here the moment the light came on indicates that they think the coin is here as well."

"What about hotel security?" Peukington asked.

"Unless someone saw you come in," Renard answered, "we're clear. No cameras at the entrances, and none in here."

"Who are these two?" Peukington nodded in our direction as he sized us up.

"They are Americans. They're staying at the hotel," Pistache joined the conversation.

Peukington grunted as he looked my direction before shifting his gaze to the pickpocket.

"Jacques Pistache," the gangster greeted him.

Janie and Trudel took a sip.

"Nice to see you again," Peukington said.

"You barely saw me the first time," Pistache smirked.

"Don't get smart. I have no patience for any of this. No one speaks anymore unless I am asking you a direct question. Especially Pistache," Peukington said, as he steadily moved toward the bar.

Janie and Trudel took another sip.

The gangster directed his attention back to Renard. "So, how are these American hotel guests involved?"

"Well, they weren't at first," Renard said calmly.

"Bad luck," Peukington muttered toward me.

Renard continued, "I think they were just looking for a fun night. But, I can't rule them out since they were apparently in the bar alone for some time before any of us showed up." He nodded toward me. "He has been behind the bar all night also. He may have found it and is hiding it."

"I didn't," I immediately said quietly. I was afraid of being accused of speaking out of turn, but the impulse to clear my name was strong.

Peukington's eyes shown as he thought. "I am tired of all this already, and I've only been here for a minute." He reached into his dark coat and produced a short-barreled pistol, sleek and black.

He held the gun in the air as he spoke, showing it off to the room. "I did not come here to have a good time. I didn't even come here to talk to any of you. All I want out of this moment is my property to be returned to me. No one will get hurt, as long as everything goes exactly as I want it to. So here's what we're going to do: no games, no tricks, just ... give ... me ... the ... coin."

Silence.

Janie was locked in on the gun. I knew she was scared, and I hated the fact that we were in this position. She's tough, but went pale as soon as Peukington produced the weapon. I stood frozen behind the bar as well. No one in the room blinked.

"Hmph," Trudel snorted and took a drink.

"Madame von Hugelstein. Something you care to say?" Peukington asked.

"Listen," she managed frankly. "I've been through a lot tonight. I've heard about you, but you don't scare me. I've lived through the occup ..."

"The occupation, yes I know," Peukington cut her off. "Trudel von Hugelstein, the amateur opera singer. I know everything about you."

"I am a professional," she snorted.

"Of course you are. Your dependence on that belief is borderline sad but completely necessary for you to continue through your pathetic existence. Do you know how I became who I am, Madame von Hugelstein?"

She stared back, offended.

Peukington continued, "Well, it sure wasn't by wishing I was successful. No, I identified what I wanted, and I went out to get it every single time. I met people like you along the way. But, do you know what happened to them? No, of course you don't because no one does. No one remembers the people who fail to accomplish anything real in their lives."

"Dick," Trudel spat.

"You know who else people don't remember? Here's your answer: anyone who stands in my way. They just fade into history. Those people probably won't even be mentioned by name in my biography. So it's time that I ask you, Trudel von Hugelstein: do you want to be someone who lets a stupid little coin be the thing that keeps them from ever being remembered?"

"I don't care if I'm in your biography or not," Trudel said with a snide tone.

Peukington looked at her for a moment, seemingly sizing her up. The entire room remained silent.

Peukington didn't let it last. Deciding that Trudel was a dead end, he raised the gun. Pointing it directly at Pistache, he cocked the hammer back.

"Jacques Pistache," Peukington began anew.

Janie and Trudel took a sip.

"Why wouldn't I shoot you right here, right now?" the gangster asked, slightly cocking his head.

"Because I don't have your coin?" Pistache answered, finally sounding nervous.

"So shooting you would do nothing?"

"That's right?" Pistache said, unsure he'd said the right answer.

Peukington raised an eyebrow.

"I mean," Pistache continued to stumble. "It wouldn't exactly do nothing; it would kill me. So you'd end my life ... obviously. But because I don't have the coin, it would mean nothing."

"So your life is meaningless?" Peukington asked.

Flustered, Pistache stammered, "Actually, yes. Meaningless ... kind of. I don't know. Pass? Next question?"

"So what's to stop me then? Let's say I love killing people. Are you giving me a free shot?"

"Uh … no?" The pickpocket changed his tone. "For a guy who said he didn't like playing games, you sure do seem to love playing this one with me."

Peukington didn't budge. "The thing is," the tall businessman said as he tilted his head slightly, "you started this whole thing when you lifted the coin off me. Truth be told, you are the only one here that I actually want to kill."

"Oh God!" Pistache exclaimed. "It won't do you any good. You'll just have a dead body and still no coin."

"It might be fun, though," Peukington said. "The world might be better off without you. You're a pest."

"Yeah maybe," Pistache pleaded. "But when you search my body for the coin, you won't find a thing. Then, you will have wasted all your time, and there will be blood everywhere. It'll be pretty bad."

A beat passed as Peukington seemed to contemplate the scene.

"Kill him anyway," Trudel added wryly. "I don't think that I would mind seeing it."

Pistache was panicking. "C'mon! Someone back me up here. Fleuse, say something. Victor!"

"How do we know you don't have it, my friend?" Victor answered. Fleuse's silent expression proved he had the same reservations that Victor had.

"Guys! I don't. You can trust me!"

"I knew you were dishonest from the moment you walked in this bar for the very first time," Victor said.

Pistache was sweating.

"You stole my watch off me tonight," Fleuse added with disappointment.

Pistache was at his wit's end. "My friends! I've only always been on your side. Fleuse, you have to know I was just having a little fun tonight. I was obviously going to give it back!"

Fleuse subtly shrugged and remained silent.

Pistache added, "I'm not the only dishonest person here, though! The American behind the bar is a thief too! He probably has it!"

"What!?" I yelled. "I do not have it!"

Peukington instantly shifted his gaze and the gun to me. I felt a wave of goose bumps as a rush of cold swept across my body. Nobody had ever pointed a gun at me before. I was officially scared.

"Are you a thief?" Peukington asked methodically.

"Yeah, he is!" Pistache accused again, quick to deflect attention.

"I'm not through with you, Pistache," Peukington added without removing his gaze from me. Pistache fell silent. "I'll ask again, and hopefully this time I won't be rudely interrupted. Are you a thief?"

"No! Of course not!" I was panicking.

"He is!" Pistache yelled despite the instruction from Peukington.

"American, you say that you don't know anything," Peukington noted coldly, ignoring Pistache.

"I don't, and I'm not a thief! I have no clue what Pistache is talking about! I'm just on vacation!" I exclaimed with my hands in the air.

"So give me the coin," Peukington stated coolly.

"I said I don't have it," I pleaded with desperation. "My wife and I were in here just to get a drink and things have gotten way out of hand."

Peukington looked analytically for a moment.

Pistache lowered his brow. "He is a liar too," he said softly. Peukington looked to Pistache.

The pickpocket continued, "I pulled this off him." He reached into his jacket pocket and pulled out the small statue from earlier in the evening. I was so nervous and flustered that it took a moment for my eyes to focus on it. It was mini Balzac.

"What is that?" Peukington asked as he kept the gun pointed at me.

"It usually sits on the shelves behind the bar," Pistache explained with an evil tone. "But, he had it in his pocket."

I barely knew him, but I was instantly feeling betrayed.

"So you lied," Peukington said to me.

"I can explain that," I stammered.

"No need," Peukington said with an eerie calm. "It will be easy to check your pockets for the coin when you are dead."

"No!" Janie interjected. "I gave it to him! As a present!"

"So you're a thief too?" Peukington asked, now addressing Janie. I felt somewhat relieved though, knowing that he hadn't moved the gun off me. "Is this some sort of criminal convention in here?!"

"No, it was just something, an innocent little gesture. Something to remember tonight by!" Janie pleaded. "We thought we would have been out of here hours ago. We would have actually been back and asleep by now. The figure was nothing. Just a little souvenir!"

"I doubt you'll be needing a souvenir to remember tonight," Peukington said with a smirk. It was as close to a smile as he'd come so far.

"It wasn't supposed to be a big deal!" she again shouted.

"Kind of feels like a big deal now, though doesn't it?" he answered.

"Well, you guys can have it back!" I started again. "See, no harm, no foul! It's not like it's worth a million euros!"

"True, but it's the entire principle of the thing," Peukington went on calmly. "Now that I know you two are criminals as well, how do I know you didn't take the coin either?"

"We didn't even know about the coin!" Janie yelled.

"Well, something tells me you didn't know about that little Balzac either when you walked in here, but you saw him and took him. Maybe you saw the coin and slipped that in to your pocket as well."

"I didn't!" I shouted.

"Believe me," Janie added. "We would have given it back and gotten the hell out of here by now."

"Yeah," I added. "I know you all say it's worth a lot, but we're on vacation. We were at the Louvre today for Christ's sake! We're not involved in some kind of international get-rich-quick scheme!"

"I'll tell you what," Peukington said. "If you give me the coin right now, you can both head off into the night and get one last drink at some all-night club. I'll even send you on your way with a few euros to pay for it."

"We don't have the coin," Janie answered, "but can we do that anyway?"

Immediately steering the focus off of us, Peukington addressed the room with a voice that shook like thunder.

"Ok, that's it. I'm not asking any more questions."

Renard finally lifted his head. It looked as if he was bracing himself for something.

"Listen American," he said to me without lowering the weapon. "You seem nice, like a little bunny. But since you apparently know nothing, I won't lose any information if I lose you. Plus, I hate bunnies."

I saw the muscles on the back of his hand twitch, and I heard the gunshot. As if shoved backwards, I felt the bar shelving thrust into my back. My spine shifted. With ears ringing, the immediate fire that comes with pain swelled so intensely that my eyes were forced closed. My knees gave way. Trying to fight my seized face, I forced an eye open just in time to see the bar rise as I sunk to the floor.

Chapter XIX.

The American bartender clumsily played the piano, but Jacques Pistache had barely noticed. He'd only been in the Bon Parisien for a few minutes, but the pickpocket's mind was on other, more important matters. He eyed the clock behind the bar. The ornate face once seemed elegant and artistic, but without the coin he thought the piece was gaudy. Someone here had to have removed the item.

"In the words of the Bard," he whispered into his glass as he took a drink and allowed his body to sway to the music. "The game is afoot."

Fleuse sat at a table, distracted by Trudel, who appropriately was having nothing to do with the man. The pretty American girl was encouraging her husband's horrible music, and Pistache felt free to roam the room and think.

Did Fleuse or Trudel have the coin? Did each one suspect the other? One or both would surely know that Jacques didn't have the coin if someone already nabbed it. So far, no silent conversations were being held through stolen glances or looks. Fleuse really seemed completely engaged by Trudel's words, and the latter seemed equally involved in her energies to keep him at bay.

Then what about the tourists? Did they have any idea what was going on? They seemed drunk. The American bartender's playing was becoming increasingly loud.

"Okay, that's enough of that!" Trudel shouted.

"Let him play!" Pistache answered, feigning interest. He had his actor shoes on.

Trudel ignored the pickpocket. "I just finished my drink, and I need another. What kind of bartender are you?"

"The tourist kind," the American said with a laugh.

"Honey, get her a drink," the pretty girl said.

Pistache's eyes darted around the room. Perhaps no one had the coin and it was hidden somewhere else. If that was the case, he didn't have a good idea of where to start looking. There were so many trinkets and nooks and crannies that the coin could almost have been anywhere.

The music stopped. "Aww," Pistache groaned, faking disappointment. "What shall I dance to now?"

"I didn't come to my favorite bar in the world tonight to not drink anything," Trudel squawked. "Here it's been closed for a few weeks and this is what I have to return to." The very sound of her voice annoyed Pistache to his core.

"He is doing his best," the hapless Fleuse remarked. The pickpocket watched him. If he had the coin, he would surely have signaled something to Pistache.

Fleuse continued, "It's better than serving ourselves."

"Is it?!" The opera singer snapped.

Everything about the woman repelled Pistache. She was entitled and devious. Worst of all, she may have been a vital distraction for a member of their team, Victor.

He decided to stir the pot. Perhaps if he engaged the two more, he'd be able to decipher if one of them had the coin.

"If you can tell me," Pistache mused to Trudel, "how to make something as simple as a martini, then I will buy your next drink."

"Go to hell," she grunted.

"That's what I thought," he answered with a leer. He was trying to see directly through the conversation and into the subtext of her speech, but she was proving unreadable. "You couldn't serve yourself if you tried."

Nothing. Pistache was beginning to be frustrated.

"Oh, I think I could take another beer," he said aloud as he thought about entirely different matters. But almost as soon as he'd absentmindedly said it, a new idea dawned upon him.

Fleuse hadn't silently signaled that he'd taken the coin. Pistache didn't believe that the clockmaker was bright enough to hide it from him anyway. The Americans likely didn't even know about the hidden object, so Trudel could really be the only one who had it.

All Pistache needed to do was put his skills to work and check her pockets for the coin. But, Trudel had had her guard up from the moment he'd arrived. The opera singer had made her distrust of him very evident with every step in the conversation. A distraction would help.

"Here's an idea," he announced, pleased with himself. "We should play a drinking game."

"We're listening," the pretty girl said smiling.

"Well," Pistache began confidently, inventing the game as he went. "I'm thinking maybe something that says 'welcome to Europe' for both of you."

The bartender's pretty wife was smiling.

"Perhaps," the pickpocket tried with the rise of an eyebrow and a look to the young woman, "something that involves the loss of clothing." The coin would be easier to find if everyone were removing clothing. Then again, the thought of a lumbering and naked Trudel made the pickpocket shudder.

"No," the tourists answered in concert.

"Okay then, new idea," Pistache improvised. "Does anyone have a deck of cards? I assure you, all clothes will stay on."

The American behind the bar began to rummage around for the item under the ineffective direction of Fleuse. Pistache looked around the room at all the players. Trudel would be his target, but he could not simply invade her personal space immediately. It was then that he noticed the pretty girl's necklace.

"Got it!" The bartender shouted proudly as he produced a shoebox, followed by a deck of cards. Pistache moved toward the man's wife.

"Perfect, let's see the cards. Everyone gather around up here." Pickpocketing is easier in crowds.

"Didn't you say you did a little magic?" the pretty girl asked. Her French was better than he'd imagined.

"I did," Pistache answered, maintaining his act. "But, card tricks aren't really my thing. That is, unless you have another card hiding behind your ear." The swift touch of the girl's chin and a wink proved enough distraction to flip the clasp on her necklace. He pocketed the prize.

"Back off, man," the temporary bartender said, oblivious to the actual circumstances. "Really, that's enough."

"Sorry, my friend," Pistache answered, acting apologetic and a little drunk. "I get carried away. Okay, here's the game. There are five of us here, so we deal out nine cards each. Jokers included."

The pickpocket dove headfirst into the explanation of his game. He was proud of the fluidity with which he was able to describe the rules, especially considering there had been no advance planning.

The instructions of the game were rather basic, and the collected group made it easy for Pistache to brush against their pockets. Obviously, he cared more about the others busying themselves than the game itself at all. Although he'd already managed the necklace from the pretty American, Trudel would still be a difficult target. He'd need every advantage.

"And the jack?" the opera singer asked, snapping Pistache's concentration.

"The jack is in the blind!" the pickpocket exclaimed, pleased with his recovery. "Whoever has the queen, produce it and drink!"

Just then, a man entered. All parties turned to see the stranger, who appeared with a pleasant look on his face.

"Good evening, sir," the American bartender said. Pistache thought the tourist was a fool, pretending to be a real Parisian bartender.

"Good evening. How about a beer?" the stranger answered.

Something was familiar about the man to Pistache, the sound of his voice, his face. Even his gait rang a bell, but he could not place the man.

"Sounds good," the American replied.

Pistache knew he had to think fast. Now that there was an uninvolved bystander in the room, could he proceed as he needed to? Did he invite him to play? Would not inviting the stranger look too suspicious?

"Looks like you are all in the middle of a card game," the man said.

"Yes," the pickpocket answered. He only had one real choice on handling this unexpected patron. The pickpocket would need to ignore the fact that the man was somewhat familiar. Devoting any more mental energy to searching his memories would be too distracting, especially if it unearthed some trivial encounter on a metro or in this very bar.

"In fact," Pistache continued. "I was just explaining the rules to my friends here. Would you like to join? It could be easily arranged."

"No, thank you."

Pistache felt relieved.

"I brought a book, so I'll be comfortable somewhere over there, thanks," the stranger finished.

Pistache refocused. It would be easy to continue with the stranger removed from the moment. As the man went to his table, Pistache maintained character and announced, "So we continue! Where's the king of spades!"

Little did he know, a game-changing move had just been made.

*   *   *

The card game progressed, and Pistache was beginning to feel as though his chances of getting close to Trudel were running out. She was becoming friendlier with drink, but as the rounds kept piling up, the game seemed to drag on.

At various points in the action, Pistache would glance in the direction of the stranger. He knew from experience to be aware of his entire surroundings, and he was unnerved when he looked the way of the man at the table. The man seemed to be peering back. Maybe it was just Pistache's imagination, but he even felt as though he detected a smirk at times.

No matter the circumstance, Pistache knew he needed to find the coin. Growing frustrated still with Trudel, he moved to Fleuse, who was looking rather weary with drink.

"Are you running out of steam, my dear man?" Pistache asked, hoping the new tactic with Trudel's suitor would change the opera singer's demeanor.

"Don't give up now," he continued. "You just need a little pick-me-up."

Pistache moved so quickly to Fleuse that the clockmaker barely had time to resist being drawn into a somewhat intimate embrace. Pistache hummed a lullaby, but kept one eye on Trudel.

The opera singer seemed mildly entertained for a moment. She took a sip of her drink and dryly commented, "You two are strange."

Fleuse protested. Pistache checked the man's pockets as they danced. Unsurprisingly, no coin. He lifted Fleuse's watch, a momentary distraction. The pickpocket couldn't help himself. The man didn't seem to notice, nor did any of the other patrons for that matter. He told Fleuse as he walked away, "You move well, my man."

"Did you like my dancing?" The clockmaker asked the opera singer softly.

"You were hating it yourself in the moment," Trudel said. "Now you are proud of it?"

"Of course he's proud," Pistache said, creeping closer to her. Sensing a change in mood, the pickpocket was ready to pounce. All he needed was a second. "We were good together just now."

"Who has the three?" the American bartender asked.

Trudel looked to her hand, and Pistache considered leaping in, but he hesitated just long enough to miss the opportunity.

"What happens if consecutive cards are in the blind?" the bartender piped up again.

Slightly annoyed, Pistache just wished the tourist would not care about the card game. Without making too much effort to pretend the game was in fact a real one, Pistache blurted out "then everyone takes a drink!" He shrugged lightly and yelled "Pistache!"

"You're making that up," Trudel said.

The pickpocket inched closer.

"Yes I am. Are you not having fun?"

"No, actually, I am."

Finally sensing an opportunity, Pistache lit up inside. "I knew it, Madame von Hugelstein!" he exclaimed. He could almost reach her handbag. But no, he knew she wouldn't put the coin there. It was too precious, and she'd know others would be looking for it. It had to be on her person.

"But," she added, holding her finger up to make an exception. "That doesn't mean I find you at all funny!"

Pistache felt as though she was almost flirting with him. It was the moment he needed.

"Madame von Hugelstein, I must tell you!" The pickpocket bellowed as he thrust his arm around her and swiftly managed his hand underneath her scarf, into her inside jacket pocket. "I have met my match!"

It was a lucky, albeit educated guess. There, inside the cozy darkness of the opera singer's breast pocket, Pistache closed his fingers around a weighty, cold piece of thin precious metal. The coin had been found.

The lift was nearly flawless as Trudel instinctively leaned away from him and ducked from beneath his arm. Pistache did everything he could to hide his elation, but after an entire evening of charades and plotting, he felt victorious. He slipped the coin into his own pocket and immediately took a drink in an attempt to hide his smile.

"Let's have a break from the game," the tourist finally announced.

"Yes, I'm good with that," his wife agreed.

"It was just getting fun!" the pickpocket exclaimed, clutching the prize in his pocket.

*   *   *

Pistache knew he couldn't leave immediately. That kind of behavior would likely arouse suspicion with Fleuse and Trudel. He assumed that Trudel hadn't left earlier for the same reason. The pickpocket had sat himself at a table with Fleuse to let his nerves calm as he planned his exit. It should seem casual, even if maybe a little abrupt.

Fleuse was droning on and on about something, completely oblivious to any subtext in the room. Trudel also seemed totally unaware of the circumstances. She thought that she still had the coin. Pistache took a quick moment to revel in his success. He quietly drank to his talents.

"Another of the same, please," the stranger ordered his drink, as he turned and once again made eye contact with Pistache.

As if a nail had been driven into his sternum, the pickpocket suddenly recognized the man. He knew in that instant that this was the man from Lavaar Peukington's party. He stood instinctively, feeling the full gravity of the situation wash over him.

As the American bartender and Peukington's man had a mindless conversation about the drinking game, Pistache was flooded with certainties about his new perspective on the situation.

This man was not here by accident. All the subtle looks and smiles from the stranger at the table throughout the evening had not been only the observations of a good-natured bystander. In fact on the contrary, Pistache was now disheartened to know that his every move had probably been watched. This man was also looking for the coin and perhaps even knew that Pistache had it.

The pickpocket knew he wasn't leaving without engaging this man somehow.

"So tell us, my friend," Pistache exclaimed, already knowing the answer. "What brings you in tonight?"

"Well, I wanted a drink. I happened to see this place as I was walking by. It looked as good a spot as any," Renard lied.

Pistache squinted at him, and a corner of the man's lip rose.

"Well, you couldn't have chosen better, my friend." Pistache weighed his options and wondered how quickly he could make it to the door. He noted that this stranger had actually placed himself in the way without appearing to threaten to anyone. Pistache tried to steer the conversation in a new direction. "What are you reading?"

"It is a book of poetry. I found it at a book fair recently."

"Very cool," the pretty girl, said.

"Oh yes? Who wrote it?" Pistache asked, never taking his eyes off the stranger. No time now to hit on the American girl.

"Various authors," the man said with a roll of his eyes, as if he knew Pistache didn't really care.

"I've never heard of him," the pickpocket answered laughing.

"I liked the picture on the cover. Poems are short. They are easy to read," Peukington's man pressed on.

"I have actually always thought the opposite. They are kind of cryptic," Pistache said. Would he be able to find any way out at all?

"That's the beauty of them. I like to search for the subtle hints at meaning," Renard answered.

"That always just frustrated me."

"Not me," he answered with a step toward Pistache. The man was glaring at the pickpocket through his own words. "It's what I do. It's like a code to decipher or a treasure to uncover. I like the hunt almost as much as I like the eventual feeling of discovery and release."

Pistache hated this man. "Aren't you a deep one?!" he roared.

The pickpocket couldn't ignore the double meaning. If it's a challenge this man wanted, then Pistache would give it to him. He continued, "Have you read one yet that you don't understand?"

"No. Eventually, I always figure them out."

Arrogant prick, Pistache thought.

The stranger picked up his drink and smiled but didn't take his eyes off of Pistache. The pickpocket had to make a move.

"Well, this brief exchange has gone on long enough without knowing each other. Jacques Pistache," he said, introducing himself through his teeth. "It's a treat to meet you, finally."

"Julian Renard, and it certainly is." Neither man sounded at all sincere.

Pistache knew that this evening was far from over.

Chapter XX.

Janie stood over me in hysterics. My eyes could barely open. The lighting was suddenly too bright. With furiously ringing ears, I somehow sensed the room raged on the other side of the bar. My entire upper body was throbbing, and the dirty floor seemed to pull at the skin on my face.

As soon as she saw my eyelids flutter, Janie exploded even further, this time with a bright look on her face. I clutched my chest at the center of the pain. I became aware that I'd been mumbling fiercely. My heart hit my chest three times harder than it ever had before.

"Honey! You're alive! Are you okay?!" Janie screamed as I felt her tears drip onto my face. I raised my hand to wipe them from my cheeks. I forced my eyelids open. For the first time, my eyes focused.

"I'm not bleeding," I rambled a few times, looking down for the source of the pain. My face felt hot. "My chest hurts. My back hurts too. My legs feel heavy." Voices rung simultaneously like bells. I couldn't tell if they were in my head or coming from the other side of the bar.

"You were shot! I thought you were dead!" Janie said through more tears. "I can't believe it."

"Where is all the blood?" I asked again as I glanced around. I craned my neck from my crumpled position on the floor behind the bar. Slowly, my equilibrium was returning to balance.

"I have no idea," she said through sniffles and nervous laughter. "It's a miracle."

I moved to sit myself up. Incredible pain, and I again grabbed my chest.

"Stay down," she said over sirens in my head. "They were fighting, but it's mostly over now."

I didn't listen. Adrenaline rushed me into a rage. Code red. I pushed myself up again, reaching directly for the rifle underneath the bar. Without thinking, I grabbed it and climbed to a standing position. My eyes focused, and Janie clung to my side, still sobbing. As quickly as I could, I clamored over sinks and glassware onto the bar top. Janie looked on in horror. From my vantage point high above the room, I took hold of the trigger, and carelessly aimed the gun at the ceiling.

BANG.

The room immediately froze. Sudden silence. My eyes had finally cleared. Peukington sat in a chair, unconscious. Pistache and Fleuse were in the middle of propping him up and tying him into a seated position. Where had they gotten rope? Another chair lay in hundreds of splintered pieces on the floor nearby. Victor was holding Renard's arms behind him, clearly struggling before I brought the room to a standstill. Trudel panted, as she clutched a wine bottle. I noticed that it wasn't broken, so I pictured her clubbing someone with it. I imagined that must have hurt. A wine bottle is a dull instrument.

A few ceiling tiles fell near me, a result of my gunshot.

"Are you positive that was necessary?" Pistache said with an eerie calmness.

"ARE YOU SERIOUS?!" I shouted at him. "That guy shot me! Do you think that I'm overreacting!?"

"Where is all the blood?" Trudel asked, echoing my initial thoughts.

"Good point," Pistache noticed. "Zombie?"

"Listen up," I said, asserting my place over the room. "My wife and I just came here for a good time tonight, but somehow we ended up in the middle of this! We have never even wanted to find this thing! It's all of you who forced us to stay! How am I the one who wound up being shot?!"

I heard Janie sniffle again, but she wasn't cowering when I looked back at her beneath me. I could tell she was mad.

"Now this has gone on long enough!" I shouted. "I probably should have found a way to get us out of here a long time ago, but I guess I've learned my lesson. I have this rifle. It's time this ends right now! Which one of you has this damn coin?!"

Still silence. They all looked at each other, waiting for someone to speak up.

"Seriously?!" I screamed. "I just got shot over this thing, and you guys still are trying to hide it from each other?!"

Still nothing.

"Really, why aren't you bleeding?" Trudel asked again.

"I don't know!" I shouted. I couldn't stop yelling. "We'll worry about that later! Seriously, who has this coin?!"

With every breath, pain shot across my chest. Again I clutched the area in which I'd been shot, but something felt different. I ran my hand over my chest, and felt a small hard object in the left front breast pocket of the old black-and-white checkered flannel from behind the bar.

Momentarily distracted from the room, I reached into the pocket and closed my hand around a small piece of metal. I removed the object, and opened my palm. There, sitting in the center of my right hand, was a gold coin.

"Oh my god," Janie whispered as she covered her mouth.

"That's the coin!" Fleuse gasped.

"How long have you had that, Peter?" Janie asked, completely shocked.

I checked my shirt and torso again, and looked back at the coin. Just as it had been described, it was scuffed with bullet markings and somehow maintained a dull, antique magnificence. For a brief moment, I truly felt as though I was holding a wealth of history in one hand. Suddenly, I believed it all unquestionably.

"I can't believe I got shot in the coin."

Fleuse stood open-mouthed. "He got shot in the coin?" He echoed.

"Do you know what this means?" Pistache said in a whisper loud enough for everyone to hear. "The Napoleon story is true."

"Of course it's true," Renard muttered.

"Is there some kind of magic linked to that thing?" Pistache muttered in disbelief.

"A historic, magic coin," Trudel muttered.

"No wonder everyone who's possessed it has been filthy rich!" Pistache mused.

Victor and Renard still stood in silence, but I noticed Peukington's man roll his eyes at the others' suggestions of magic.

"Honey," Janie started. "Seriously, how long have you had that?"

"I ... I have no idea," I stammered, finally able to lower my voice.

"He's been hiding it the entire time!" Fleuse exclaimed.

"Or maybe the coin is cursed," Trudel added, still lost in thought. "This is not the first time that someone has been shot with the coin in their pocket."

"Don't be an idiot," Pistache snapped. "It's not like they die."

"Well true," she answered. "But it drives people around it crazy. Look at all of us! We've been mad over this thing for weeks! Monsieur Peukington shot this tourist over it." She looked toward Renard. "Does he do that often? Shoot people?"

Renard thought for a moment. "Actually sometimes, yes."

"Huh. I was hoping that wasn't ordinary behavior," she answered.

"You American rat," Victor grunted at me. "Stealing from my bar." He was clearly not buying the magic coin discussion. Either that, or the magic coin was cursing him and driving him mad to the point that he couldn't pay attention to the idea.

"I didn't steal anything from your bar!" I shouted.

"Except that little guy that your wife took," Pistache pointed out.

"I know a thief when I see one," Victor hissed.

"Didn't you steal the coin in the first place?" I sharply retorted.

"Yes, he did," Renard snapped.

There was a moment of silence as everyone digested the situation.

I looked down at the coin in my palm again. For the first time, I pictured myself sipping a martini on the plane ride home, sitting first class. "I'm going to be rich!" I whispered to myself from my spot on top of the bar.

Janie was watching silently until my daydream became obvious. "Honey, please."

"Do the right thing here." Renard snapped, finally wrestling out of Victor's grip. The old bartender didn't try to restrain him. "Give me that coin, and we'll be all set."

"What makes you think we're letting you leave with that?" Pistache asked Peukington's man. "You are severely outnumbered."

Renard ignored him. "I assume that you will return it to its rightful owner. Besides, you said you didn't even want the coin."

"Well, I didn't," I countered. "But, excuse me for feeling like you all owe me something. I'm the guy that got shot on vacation in the middle of your whole mess!"

"Well, the coin protected you," Pistache said. "So it's really nothing, right?"

"Nothing!? Are you kidding me?!" I exploded.

"It's not nothing," Renard conceded, taking a deep breath. "Monsieur Peukington is very sorry about that."

"Sorry?! What's to stop me from calling the police right now about this whole thing?! In fact," I thought aloud as I looked at Janie, "I probably should call the cops, right?"

"Yeah. Actually, how have they not shown up yet?" Janie wondered aloud. "Especially after a couple gun shots."

"Actually, no one's calling the police," Renard said. "Monsieur Peukington will not be found at a crime scene."

"You know, Renard," Pistache interjected. "The guy is going to be found pretty much anywhere Fleusie and I decide to leave him right now."

Renard rolled his eyes again. "Okay, enough. Untie him please," he said as he took a step toward the unconscious man in the chair.

Victor reached out and grabbed Renard's shoulder. Trudel lifted the wine bottle, and Peukington's man backed down.

Victor hissed at Renard, "You may have thrown me off a bridge, but I got you now. And I have these two to help if I need it."

I had a tough time believing that Fleuse and Pistache had ever been too much help in a fight.

"Peukington stays in the chair," Victor said frankly.

"I know he's supposed to be somebody," I added cautiously, "but he did shoot me. I think we really have to call the police."

"C'mon. What a rookie," Pistache muttered, tightening up the tie-up job on Peukington. "You don't see any of us diving for the phone do you?"

Everyone ignored the question.

"An unfortunate act," Renard said through gritted teeth. "One that renders you deserving of compensation, I imagine. Monsieur Peukington will absolutely want to see you cared for, in exchange for your discretion of course. And the coin."

I looked at Janie. She raised her eyebrow.

"If you are offering to buy it back from me, then let's make a deal," I said, trying to hide my fear of the situation. "Otherwise, I'll just keep the coin. That would be compensation enough."

Renard shook his head, and the others in the room all made various sounds of exasperation.

"I thought you didn't want the coin," Renard said.

"Well I didn't, at first. Then, I GOT SHOT."

"You have no claim to it," Pistache blurted out, ignoring me. "The rest of us have been grappling over this thing for weeks."

"Excuse me?!" Renard leapt a little as he spoke to Pistache. "Are you insinuating that the rest of you have a legitimate claim to the coin?! You stole it!"

"Well this American idiot shouldn't walk out of here with it!" Pistache yelled back.

"He's not going to. Everybody take it easy!" Victor jumped in.

"Wait!" I yelled over everyone. "What makes you think I'm not leaving with the coin? I have a gun. I'm pretty much doing whatever I want right now!"

The room was quiet for a moment.

"Your gun is useless, barkeep," Victor said calmly.

"What do you mean?"

"It's a single shot rifle," Renard answered for Victor. "It's just a prop now."

Feeling silly, I sighed. My entire upper body ached with the breath. I managed, "Oh, okay."

"Come on down here, honey," Janie said reaching for my hand. At least I'd stopped the brawl earlier.

"So," I announced in a much less threatening tone as I descended the bar top. "Thank you to whomever wailed on this Peukington guy with a chair. Based on the broken one on the ground, I assume that's what happened."

Trudel spoke up. "That was actually your wife."

I looked to Janie. "Seriously?"

"Well, he shot you. I lost my mind," Janie said with a shrug.

"It was pretty awesome, actually," Trudel added.

"Quite a girl," Pistache said.

"Oh, okay," I said. "Wow, honey." We moved out from behind the bar. "Well, should we call an ambulance or something? I mean, Monsieur Peukington probably needs medical attention, so ..."

"Who cares if he needs medical attention? He didn't care about killing you," Janie answered coldly.

"I hate to leave you all," Pistache interrupted without too much grace. "But I believe the night has dragged on long enough." He turned to me. "Bartender, give me the coin and I'll be on my way."

"Gimme a break, man," I said in English with a subtle laugh. "After all this, why would I just hand it over?"

"Because," he answered as he reached into his sport coat pocket. "You have to."

I heard the 'click' as Pistache cocked the revolver. My heart sank. It went without need for explanation that he'd removed it from Lavaar Peukington at some point during the struggle.

"And this one isn't out of ammunition," Pistache added mockingly.

Renard sighed and took a step backward.

"Wait, Jacques," Victor managed.

Pistache didn't move. I was frozen, immediately aware that there was a chance I was about to get shot for the second time in a night. Janie arrived silently at my side.

Victor continued as he stepped forward, "It's not real."

Momentarily distracted from the coin, Pistache answered, "What do you mean it's not real. The coin's a fake?"

"No, the coin is very real. It's authentic absolutely, but the story isn't."

"Napoleon never owned it?" Trudel asked, echoing the thoughts of the room.

"What is going on here?" A voice suddenly awoke. Every head turned. Peukington sat in the chair with his head up.

"When did you wake up?" Pistache said in a sarcastically cheery tone.

Peukington looked around. "What happened?"

Janie took a step forward and spoke very seriously. "You shot my husband. So, I beat your ass with a chair."

I smiled, but tried not to let Peukington see it.

"Wow," Trudel said. "Look out for her, am I right?"

"You're still mad about that?" Pistache asked Janie in jest.

She shot him a look. "Same thing is going to happen to you if you shoot him too," she answered with a nod to the revolver. Pistache was still pointing it at me.

"What happened here?" Peukington repeated. "Where is the coin? Renard, untie me!"

No one moved.

"Julian," Pistache said without breaking his stare at me. "Save your breath. I'll fill the rich man in."

"Renard, get me out of here," Peukington hissed. He didn't notice that Victor still stood closely behind Renard.

"So you shot this poor American tourist," Pistache began for Peukington. "... And then his wife kicked your ass with a chair. At least that was her description."

"I said that I beat his ass with a chair," Janie said. "You can't kick an ass with a chair. How are you supposed to kick with a chair?"

Pistache thought for a moment. "Funny. Anyway, we tied you up so you wouldn't try to murder anyone else while your lackey here traded fisticuffs with our former bartender. He's a tough bird. While all that was happening, this tourist guy here comes back from the dead. It turns out that he's had the coin all along. So that's something. Anyway, here we are now. He was about to give it over to me when Victor and Julian here decide to tell me that it's worth nothing."

"Like hell it's worth nothing," Peukington spit. "It belonged to Napoleon."

"If you believe in fairy tales," Victor answered with soft hiss.

Pistache ignored Victor. "That's what I told them, Peuky. If it's worth nothing, then why did everyone show up here tonight for it?"

"Exactly," Peukington agreed. "For once, pickpocket, we are in complete agreement. How about you untie me now."

"Nice try," Pistache said with a smile.

"Renard!" Peukington exclaimed. "Get me out of here! Grab that coin, and let's go. Enough monkeying around."

Victor silently moved to Peukington. Without a word, the old bartender wound up and delivered a swift and powerful fist to Peukington's face. The businessman once again slumped and fell into silence.

Trudel and Fleuse jumped back a little. Janie and I were stunned.

"Victor?!" Trudel shrieked.

Renard rolled his eyes, and Victor looked back at him.

"What?" The bartender asked Peukington's man. "It's not like he was actually helping anything here. I got thrown off a bridge, and that American guy got shot! He's better off knocked out!"

Renard sighed. "It's going to be so much harder to convince him not to kill you now."

Chapter XXI.

Victor Laquer was still not ready to be seen. He glided along familiar streets and felt a subtle sense that he didn't belong. Almost two weeks had passed. Sarah had been more than accommodating, but he'd needed to join the world of the living again. Walking through the town he knew, he felt as though something had changed. It was as if Paris no longer belonged to him.

Victor pushed his way through a park, passing a long string of bicycles chained to a fence. A small flock of birds parted on the path as he walked by, annoying a woman with birdseed on a bench.

Just outside the park, Victor glanced at his reflection in the windows of a café he knew well. He saw a face wracked with worry. Once he arrived at the Bon Parisien, he figured he could say hello to the management, apologize, probably pick up one last check, of course see if the coin was still there, and get out of town. He thought of Fleuse and Jacques. Trudel knew about their secret as well. Did she find a way to get herself wrapped up in this mess? What about the man who'd thrown him off a bridge?

Victor took a turn one street early. It wasn't a shortcut, but the path up the alleyway afforded a glimpse from a distance of the Hôtel des Bretons. He enjoyed approaching the bar this way. The archway at the end of the alley perfectly framed the Bon Parisien's windows across the street.

But today, Victor noticed something was different. At the end of the alley, a dark shadow blocked Victor's view of the hotel. It was a character.

At first, the bartender assumed it was just another Parisian leaning up against a wall on the sidewalk, rolling his own cigarette. But as he approached the person's backside, something was different. He could tell there was no cigarette. In fact, the character's body was rigid and alert. He was watching for something and was transfixed by the Hôtel des Bretons. Victor immediately softened his step, recognizing the man who'd thrown him from a bridge. Victor quietly approached Julian Renard.

Without thinking, he seized the man's jacket and whipped him around, pressing him into the brick alleyway wall. With Victor's hands firmly around Renard's neck, Peukington's man both choked and gasped with surprise at once.

"Victor!" He managed in pain.

"That's right, motherfucker."

"But I threw you off the bridge. You're alive!"

"I'm back from the dead," Victor snapped as he couldn't control his temper.

Renard struggled for breath, still pinned.

"Why on Earth should I not kill you right now?!" Victor yelled as he reinforced his grip on Peukington's henchman.

"Keep your voice down!" Renard hissed in pain. "I'm hiding here."

Ignoring him Victor answered, "Let's hear it. Give me one reason."

Renard squirmed. "We'll make a deal!"

"You think you can buy me off? Really? After throwing me off a bridge?!"

"Listen," Renard struggled. "You chose to play this game. Getting thrown off a bridge, or worse, is part of the risk you take. Let go of me, and let's work this out."

Victor thought for a moment, but didn't relent. "What can you offer me?"

"No, no, no," Renard squirmed, grabbing Victor's hands. "You've got it all wrong. The question is, what can you offer me?"

"Are you serious!?" Victor again was yelling. "I'm the one with his hands on your throat. You think you're in a position to negotiate?"

Renard winced and grunted, tightening his grip on Victor's wrists. "I bested you once old man. Do you have enough fight in you to try again?"

Victor knew that if he tried to out-muscle Renard, he'd lose the fight.

Renard continued, seemingly sensing weakness. "So I'll ask again, what are you going to do for me?"

The bartender released the man, and took a step back.

"What the hell are you talking about? Why would I do anything for you?"

Renard fixed his sport coat and cleared his throat. "That's better. First things first: How are you?"

"Cut the shit," Victor spat, slightly short of breath. "Just answer the damn question. Why would I do anything for you?"

"Well let's see," he answered. "I already killed you once, and frankly, I'm not afraid to do it again."

Victor winced.

"So," Peukington's man continued as he gestured toward the Bon Parisien. "Right now all your friends are in that bar. I don't know what's happened yet, because no one has come out. That tells me that they either can't find the coin in there, or they are arguing over who gets to keep it."

Victor craned his neck to see into the bar's windows, but he couldn't make out the details.

"So unless you have a better idea," Renard said, "here's my plan. I would like to kill you again, drag your body in there, and remind them what happens to people when they take things that belong to other people. Specifically, Lavaar Peukington."

Victor's shoulders dropped. "Okay," he answered with a deflated tone. "Counter offer. I just run away. You never hear from me again."

"Well that's a nice thought," Renard said. "But, Monsieur Peukington will always want me to hunt you down. That's the kind of man he is. Are you willing to live your life with a target on your back? Can you hide out forever?"

Victor felt as though he'd already lost. "Okay, what can I do?"

"Here's what's going to happen," Renard answered calmly. "I'm going in there. If anyone comes out other than me, you get the coin from them. I don't care how."

Victor nodded.

"If an hour or so goes by and I haven't come out," Renard continued, "then you have my permission to come in, but only under one stipulation."

"What's that?"

"Not only do none of them know that you are alive, but they don't know that we're making a deal. They'll be surprised, but they can't know that we talked. They have to believe that you are still working as a team with Fleuse and Jacques."

"So what happens if I get the coin?" Victor asked.

"Simple. You can give it to me, and as a reward, I'll tell Peukington not to kill you."

"Will he listen to you?"

"You had better hope that he does," Renard answered with a laugh. "Listen, Monsieur Peukington is a businessman. He will recognize this deal. I can't say he'll be so lenient with your friends."

Victor thought for a moment. "What happens if someone kills you in there?" Victor asked.

"Really!?" Renard asked, entertained. "Do you think someone in there is capable of that?"

"You never know," Victor said coldly.

"In that event," Renard mused, "You'll have to return the coin to Monsieur Peukington yourself and explain our arrangement. The only other outcome is you getting thrown off another bridge or something."

"I guess I really hope that no one kills you," Victor mused with a defeated shrug.

"Good plan," Renard said. "Where have you been, anyway?"

"Why would I tell you," Victor asked. "If something goes awry, I'm going to need a hiding place. You didn't even know I was alive."

"But, I wasn't looking. Trust me, when Lavaar Peukington wants to find somebody, he always does. Dead or alive."

Victor looked again at the bar, and then to Renard. "Fine. I'm still not telling you, though."

"I can live with that," Renard laughed. "Hang on to that if it makes you feel better. So, are you ready?"

"One last thing," Victor added.

"Go ahead," Renard said.

"I'm going to hit you when I get in there."

Renard clenched his teeth. "Don't do anything stupid. You need me on your side, bartender."

"I'm not asking. If we have to pretend this conversation never took place in front of all of them, I'm going to have to really sell it. And I'm pretty annoyed that you threw me off a bridge, so an apology would be great at some point."

Renard waited a moment and extended his hand. "Victor, I'm glad you aren't dead. Now let's go finish this thing, huh?"

"Don't patronize me," Victor grunted. "Save the act for the bar."

"If things were different," Renard continued undeterred, "I sincerely believe that I would have enjoyed a whiskey with you."

Victor averted his gaze, but shook the man's hand anyway. "Yeah," he answered.

"See you soon, my friend." Renard buttoned his sport coat and crossed the street for the Hôtel des Bretons.

*   *   *

The safe hit the floor with a thud. Pistache could feel himself starting to sweat. Once it was discovered that he held the coin, there's no telling what Renard would do. As long as the safe remained locked, Pistache assumed that Renard would be preoccupied and the pickpocket would be out of harm's way. It would buy him time to strategize.

Just as he was thinking it, he heard Renard splinter the leg of a chair as he wedged it against the combination dial. Pistache looked up from the card game.

"That didn't work," Fleuse said.

"That's true, Monsieur Newman. Thank you," Renard said, annoyed.

"I am going to need another drink," Pistache thought out loud. He didn't realize that his glass was empty as he taught the pretty American girl the Sailor's Revenge. She was still attempting the move, and Pistache found her clumsiness charming. The girl was catching on slowly, though.

Of course, none of this had changed the fact that he still needed an exit strategy. He'd slowly come to terms with the fact that he wasn't going to be able to simply walk out of the place with the coin. He needed to re-hide it somewhere. Preferably, somewhere out of the way. And to do it, he might need a distraction. He had the answer almost as soon as he'd begun thinking about it.

"Wait a minute!" he exclaimed to the American bartender. "Can you make a Feu du Saint Denis?"

"I have no idea what that is," the tourist answered. His French pronunciation was laughable.

"It's a flavored whiskey shot, but the top of it is on fire," Pistache excitedly announced. He knew it was a little risky, but fire causes chaos. He needed that to guarantee that no eyes were on him.

"Who was Saint Denis?" the American asked.

Pistache had no idea. Who cares? "He was a saint."

"Huh, okay," the American answered, looking unfulfilled. "Let's try and keep the lighting of fires to an absolute minimum."

"Well, think about it," Pistache pressed on. What if there was a way to somehow use the fire to open the safe?" He knew that fire might damage the safe, which would be in his favor. If it was never opened, the coin in his pocket might stay a secret.

"That's a terrible idea," Renard said, overhearing the conversation.

"Why not? Maybe we weaken something that can give way in the lock," Pistache tried.

"Or wind up melting it shut," Fleuse added.

Damn you Fleuse, Pistache thought.

"Fleuse is right," Trudel said as she looked over her hand of cards.

"Thank you," Fleuse said with a smile at Trudel.

"Well for whatever it's worth, I don't love it either," the pretty American girl said.

Pistache noticed her absentmindedly flipping the bottle cap between her fingers. "No one asked you, American. Go back to working on your bottle cap trick." He looked to Trudel. "Keep your new friend quiet."

Pistache felt the bottle cap lightly hit his arm. He remembered how much he hated most American girls.

"Well, it looks like your chair thing is working really well," the pickpocket went on sarcastically. "So, maybe you should keep going with that while I make a Feu du Saint Denis for everyone here who likes me."

"Let's just hear him out for a second," Fleuse surprisingly suggested. "Okay Jacques, what do you propose?"

The pickpocket was pleased. He asked the tourist, "Do you mind if I join you?"

"No, come on back."

Feeling his victory closer at hand, Pistache ventured behind the bar. As he explained the dangers of poison du poisson, his eyes darted between the bottles. The hiding place for the coin should not be in plain site this time, he thought.

Pistache lined up the shot glasses, always keeping an eye on Renard. He lit the drink, immediately realizing that he needed more fire. If a distraction was really going to work, the situation must truly be out of control.

As everyone drank, Fleuse added, "Let's see just how hot this booze burns and its effect on intricate metalwork. We might be able to tell if it will cause more harm than good. We can use my watch."

Pistache couldn't believe his luck. Here someone else had perfectly set up a dangerous-sounding situation. In that brief moment, the pickpocket wondered if Fleuse could actually hear his thoughts.

As some voiced their objections, Pistache watched Renard. He was consumed with the safe but not inattentive to the happenings at the bar. The pickpocket continued his plan undeterred. He was sure that Renard would not catch him with the coin. As Fleuse laid his timepiece out on the bar, Pistache liberally dumped the booze all over it.

"Okay, hang on," the tourist said. "You can't light that now. You'll ignite the whole place."

"So?" Pistache couldn't help laughing. That might actually be handy. If he burned the bar down, he might be able to disappear into the night with the coin.

The American bartender continued to protest but finally caved in. He stood at the ready with wet towels as Pistache threw a lit match on to the bar.

It wasn't enough, and Pistache was disappointed. The situation was not nearly chaotic enough to keep Renard from noticing Jacques as he handled the coin. The American bartender jumped in with a towel, but the pickpocket was determined. He threw the towel back at the American, and poured more booze over the flames. The pickpocket really needed to go for the gold.

Bingo. The bar top practically exploded.

"Jesus, are you crazy?!" the American yelled.

"Honey, your arm!" The pretty girl shouted as her husband's shirt caught fire.

The American bartender jumped in front of the pickpocket to douse his sleeve in a sink. Pistache dove out of the way, and simultaneously slipped the coin into the front pocket of Victor's old shirt behind the bar. Peukington's man never saw him. The deed was done.

"Smooth, Jacques," Fleuse muttered sarcastically.

He didn't know how right he was, the pickpocket thought.

Chapter XXII.

Pistache took a step toward me, rededicated to aiming the gun in my direction. I tried to focus my eyes on the barrel, but all the night's alcohol kept my vision from working properly.

"I see what you're trying to do here, Victor," Pistache said with an icy stare in my direction. "You think that by telling me the coin is worth nothing, I'll just walk out of here."

"It's worth nothing," Victor said flatly.

"Do you think you're saving this American's life?" The pickpocket said. "I call your bluff. If you'd known the coin was worthless, you wouldn't have come back here tonight."

Everyone looked to Victor. The former bartender sighed and admitted, "Okay, well it's not worth nothing. But, it's not worth one million euros."

Finally, Pistache broke his stare. "I'm through with taking your word for it. When this tourist hands me the coin, I'll get a second opinion."

Victor grunted in defeat.

"Nice try, friend," Renard said to the old bartender.

"I'm not your friend," Victor snapped.

"Don't forget," Renard hissed. "You need me."

Pistache interrupted their sidebar. "Maybe it's just worth a little, and maybe it's worth a lot. Either way, it's time, American. I'll take it now and be on my way."

I stared into the pickpocket's eyes. His look was unwavering, and his hand was steady. Concluding that he might actually pull the trigger, the coin suddenly felt heavier in my sweaty palm.

"Go ahead, honey," Janie said softly to me. I'm not sure if anyone else heard. I looked at her, and she seemed to have a reassuring, confident gaze. The last thing I wanted to do was bring her any more distress.

I took one last glance at the coin, and flipped it in the pickpocket's direction. As it spun away from me in the air, I saw my dreams of riches go with it. It had been fun being a millionaire, if only for a moment.

He flawlessly caught it with his non-gun-wielding hand and immediately pocketed it inside his jacket. Janie smiled sympathetically at me.

"Thank you very much!" The pickpocket said pleasantly as he instantly stashed the gun as well. "How about one last drink for the road, tourist? A toast in celebration, really."

I didn't move.

"What exactly are we celebrating?" Trudel asked irreverently.

"Me, obviously," the pickpocket answered.

"I'll pass," Victor hissed.

"Suit yourself, old man." Pistache shrugged and swiftly moved to the bar area as everyone stood by watching. Snagging a random whiskey bottle from the myriad of glassware that we'd left on the bar at various points in the evening, he poured himself a highball.

Janie winced. "Eww."

"What?" Pistache asked.

"Um … you're not even going to use a clean glass?"

"My dear, I'm not that worried about it," Pistache exclaimed with a cheery tone. "After all. I'm rich now."

"Where are you going to go, Pistache?" Renard violently snapped.

Pistache smirked and laughed as he took a sip. He didn't answer further.

"Do you think we won't find you?" Renard added.

"Actually, yes. I do not think that you'll find me," the pickpocket answered. "See, this time I won't have these two to share the prize with."

Victor stood in silence.

Fleuse hadn't said anything in quite a while. He listened to the verbal sparring and occasionally shifted his gaze to Peukington's body in the chair.

"Cheer up, Fleusie," Pistache sneered. "I'll send you a few euros from my beach-front hut in South America."

"Fitting, I guess," Renard said. "One of your friends here already sold you out. Seems right you'd do the same."

"Like I was given a choice," Victor answered snidely. The others seemed to already know, or at least didn't seem to care.

"I'll put it to you," Renard continued to Pistache. "Hand me that coin right now, Jacques, and you walk out of here without a care in the world."

Pistache huffed in amusement. "I'm already walking out of here without a care in the world," he said as he took another drink.

"I'd say you're walking out of here carelessly. There's a difference," Renard said as he walked toward the bar. He grabbed a glass and poured himself a little brandy. "Just ask your friend here."

Victor huffed softly.

"Let me save you all the trouble," Pistache said with a grand gesture. He had the gun back in hand. "You throw Victor off a bridge, and that's supposed to scare me? Let me tell you. Jacques Pistache has been thrown off a bridge before. Actually, more than once."

"Why am I not surprised?" Trudel muttered.

"I know everything you are about to tell me," the pickpocket continued for Renard, "and I get it. You'll hunt me down. Blah blah blah."

Renard just stared.

"Come find me if you can," Pistache continued. "I showed up at that party unafraid, and I'm not afraid now either."

"If that's the way you'd like it to be," Renard said plainly.

"As for the rest of you," Pistache took another drink. "Our goodbyes can be more cordial." He looked around the room and settled on the old bartender. "Victor, I don't blame you for taking Renard up on his deal to walk free. You've got some fight in you, but you are a numbers guy. Don't get discouraged, you're not meant for this kind of stuff."

Victor looked at the ground.

"You ran a good ship here," Pistache went on. "This American guy here did alright, but you were the crown jewel of the Bon Parisien. I trust it'll never be the same, but I won't be here to find out."

"If you ever do come back," Victor answered, "these guys will be waiting. And, so will I."

"I don't doubt it, friend," Pistache answered, not sounding threatened by the former bartender. He turned to the opera singer. "As for you Trudel, I'm sorry that I never got to hear you sing."

"Rot in hell," she snapped.

The pickpocket smiled. "From one performer to another, I think you should keep at it. You might make it one day."

Trudel took a drink and stared at the man with distaste.

"As for you two," Pistache said with a turn to Janie and me. "You're okay, American. I don't detest you. And if I may say so, your wife is beautiful."

Janie rolled her eyes.

"My little flower," Pistache said as he danced toward Janie. "If you'd met me before him, I assume things would have been different."

"Right," Janie said.

"Send me off with a soft embrace," he said as he opened his arms to her.

Much to my surprise she actually leaned in and gave him a small hug with a pat on his back. When Pistache lingered, she shifted awkwardly. Finally raising her eyebrows and rolling her eyes again, she sighed, "Okay, Pistachio. That's enough." Leaning away, she shook her head and shot me a smirk.

He smiled as he backed off. "That was all I needed, my sweetheart," he said. "Travel safely on your way home, and always think of me when you think of Paris."

I scoffed. "Get the hell out of here, man."

The pickpocket turned to Fleuse. "And Monsieur Newman, what more is there to be said?"

Fleuse stood silently.

"Like I said, cheer up. I'll see you again someday. We've been through so much, and I'll always count you among my closest and best friends."

"Okay, Jacques," the clockmaker managed.

"Of course," Pistache continued, "I'm very sorry that you'll have to find a new jewel man. I think you'll discover that my talents are not easily replicated in others, but I believe that you will make do somehow. Good luck, my friend."

"Sure," Fleuse said without luster. He was clearly offended by Pistache's betrayal.

"Everyone, check to make sure you still have your watches before he goes," Renard jabbed. He sounded like he was kidding, but I absolutely checked my watch and wallet.

"Good one, Renard. I'll miss you too," Pistache said before addressing us one last time. "So that's it, everyone."

He dramatically finished the last drop of his drink. He winced and looked at the bottom of his empty glass. "Well, it was no Esprit de la Nuit!" He tossed it into the wasteland of broken tables and chairs. It shattered as it landed, piercing the quiet that had settled over the room.

The pickpocket moved to the curtain. Turning to the rest of us, he patted the coin through his coat pocket and took one last deep breath of satisfaction.

"Adieu, mes amis," he said as he theatrically opened the curtain. And in another flourish, Pistache and the coin were gone.

*   *   *

The group stood in silence for several moments, exchanging looks and digesting the finality of the events. My head was spinning. I knew it would hurt in a few short hours. I couldn't believe how much booze we'd consumed. How were we still standing?

"So that's it?" Trudel asked.

"It's over," Victor said.

"Not for me," Renard said with a shrug.

"Is Peukington going to come after us?" Trudel asked.

"No," Renard answered. "At least as long as none of you help Jacques from here on out."

"We don't even know that guy," I said.

"You have the least to worry about, tourist," Renard said.

"Thank god. Why's that?" I asked.

"Because," Janie said with a brave step forward, "this guy shot you." She nodded at the chair. "Not to mention, he did it in front of five people."

"Well, luckily," Renard answered her, "no one is hurt. That being said, Monsieur Peukington appreciates your silence on this entire matter." He'd begun untying the unconscious man. As soon as he did, Peukington moaned and shifted in the chair.

"What happened?" Peukington groaned.

"I'll fill you in, sir," Renard answered as he helped him to his feet.

"Where's Jacques Pistache?"

Janie and Trudel took a sip.

"Like I said, I'll fill you in, sir. But in the meantime, we have to get you out of here."

"Where's the coin?" Peukington grunted.

Renard didn't answer him as he hoisted the man's arm around his shoulder and neck. The two started for the curtain. Peukington stumbled with nearly his full weight on Renard. When they reached the doorway, they both leaned heavily on the frame as Peukington's man turned his head.

"Remember," Julian Renard said. "We appreciate your silence. Stay away from Jacques Pistache."

Janie and Trudel took another sip.

Renard swept the curtain aside and the men limped through.

Everyone remained silent for several seconds and finally exhaled when it was evident that they were gone. I took a look around the bar. The place was trashed.

"We are in so much trouble, honey," I said to Janie.

"Maybe we should slip out before the concierge starts for the day? We'll tell him that we left before any of this happened."

"That's not a half-bad idea," I said.

"Well, I think I'll call it a night," Victor said, walking toward the bar. He began raking up as many of his coins as he could carry. "If everyone is done stealing things for the night, I think I'll take what's left of my coin collection with me."

"Here, I can help you," I offered.

"Don't touch anything," the old bartender snapped. "I can take care of it myself."

We all watched as he stuffed his pockets and finally turned toward the curtain.

"Where the hell are you going?" Trudel said.

"I'm disappearing. I don't trust those guys for one second not to try and come after me."

"They said they're after Jacques, not us," Fleuse said.

"Still," Victor said, "I'm not taking my chances. I'm making myself scarce."

"Don't you think you owe me an explanation?!" Trudel screamed.

"Trudie," he snapped. "They threw—"

"I got it," she snapped. "They threw you off a bridge. Who cares? You didn't die or anything. What about us?!"

"No thanks," Victor said coldly. "See you around, Fleuse," he said with a nod. He parted the curtain and walked through. I doubted that the Hôtel des Bretons would ever see their bartender again.

Tears began to swell in Trudel's eyes, but she didn't let the emotion take her. There was a moment of silence, before she composed herself.

"I, too, will be leaving," she managed.

"Trudel," Fleuse said.

"Oh god," she said with an exasperated tone. "What?"

"Please let me take you to dinner."

"Dinner?! Fleuse, it's almost breakfast time."

"Anything, madame," he answered.

She thought for a moment, and looked at Janie and me before answering him.

"You may walk me down the street toward a café. I'll decide when we get there if I'm going in," she said with her nose in the air.

Fleuse was very pleased. They started for the curtain before Trudel turned around.

"One more thing, American."

"Yes?" I asked.

"How did you get the coin?"

I looked to Janie.

"I have no idea. Truly I don't. I checked the shirt earlier, and I swear it wasn't there."

"Well, if we're retracing steps, you all must suspect that I removed it from the clock," she admitted.

"When?" Fleuse asked.

"Before you arrived. I was going to leave, but you showed up too soon. I have no idea when I lost it, though," the opera singer said.

"Jacques," the clockmaker sighed.

"God, I hate impressionists," Trudel grunted. They turned, Fleuse pulled back the curtain for her, and he followed her through it.

Janie and I were finally alone again in the room.

"So," Janie said. "This has been fun!"

"I can't believe I got shot."

Janie came over to hug me. "I can't believe you're not even hurt," she said.

"Maybe I should go to the hospital or something. Just to be sure."

"Let's just go get some breakfast and let this night sink in."

I nodded. In truth, I was starving and feeling drunk. As we walked toward the curtain, I turned to take one last look back at the wreckage. The bar looked just as beautiful to me as it had the first time I'd seen it twenty-four hours earlier. We poked our heads through the curtain to scout the area and scurried to the door unseen.

Chapter XXIII.

Outside the Hôtel des Bretons, morning light gently crept over the city neighborhood.

"Were we really in there all night?" Janie asked.

"Guess so," I answered. We began to walk toward the river. Twelve hours in the Bon Parisien was already fading into memory. Somewhere deep in my skull, a small headache was gently sparking to life.

"I can't believe that just happened," Janie muttered with a little laugh. She must not have been feeling the drinks the way I was.

"I know."

Café lights made the sidewalk glow in the next block. "Let's stop up there," I added.

"No, let's put off breakfast just a bit longer. We could watch the sunrise over the river from the Pont des Arts."

Despite my hunger and the tiny headache, I let the moment win my attention. "You're right. When are we going to be able to do that again?" We turned to pass through the Tuileries.

Fine stones on the path crunched softly underfoot. For the first time, I realized exactly how exhausting the all-nighter had been. Shadows along the ground and in the trees exaggerated dimension. Colors seemed abstract and inexact. Lack of sleep does that. This was the same feeling from the morning before as I looked out our window. Paris is perfect for that type of surrealism. You know it's really out there, but you can't believe it.

We arrived at the bridge, hearing the wooden planks knock under our feet. Listening to the rhythm of our steps mingle with the lapping of small river ripples beneath, Janie and I made it to the center of the bridge without exchanging a word. We rested our elbows on the rails.

Sunlight was visible as a gentle glow, still under the horizon. Silhouettes of structures created a jagged line between city and sky.

Gradually, the light grew and turned up the heat on the navy blue morning. We only needed to wait for a few quiet minutes before the sun peeked over the ancient city like a match being struck in the distance, and the Seine was seared white with its reflection.

"I can't believe we made it," I said.

"I know," Janie answered.

"There were points in the night when I didn't believe we'd get to see this."

"I know," she said again with a nod.

I threw my hands up. "And you know what?"

"What?"

"I forgot to take the gift you stole for me from the bar."

"The little Balzac?"

"Yeah," I uttered. "Feels like that happened days ago."

"I wouldn't worry about it." Sunrise light made Janie's face glow, but she was beaming anyway. "It doesn't matter. I got you something else."

"Okay?" I asked, unsure of what she could possibly have taken.

Janie stuffed her hand into her pocket and fished something out. When she opened her palm, my stomach turned and my eyes popped. There it sat, a piece of Paris with near mythological history. The much-sought-after trophy during our bender at the Bon Parisien rested in my wife's tiny little hand. She had Peukington's coin.

"Jesus!" I yelled as I jumped. "Where the hell did you get that? How did you …?" My voice failed me.

"Pistache never should have taught me the Sailor's Revenge," she said with a sly smile.

I was speechless.

"And he never should have offered to hug me before he left," she added.

I frantically looked up and down the bridge, believing Renard or Peukington himself would leap out of nowhere to hurl us over the side. Luckily, we were alone.

"I don't believe this, honey," I stammered. My disbelief took a few moments to fully sink in. I searched my memory for the moment of Janie's lift. I suddenly remembered it all: the hug, her look, and her shift.

"Plus, he really doomed himself in the end," she continued.

"How's that?"

"So, I watched him make that last drink as he said his goodbyes."

"The one with the dirty glass? So what?"

"No one noticed," Janie continued, "but he emptied the bottle of poison du poisson into that glass and downed it right in front of us."

"The crazy stuff that makes you black out?"

"Yep. He said it himself. It looks and tastes like normal whiskey. He'll have no idea what happened tonight. He might not even realize that he thinks he left with the coin in the first place."

"Oh my god, Janie." I muttered, staring back off into the sunrise. "If they find out we have it, they're going to kill us. I love you, but you realize they're going to come after us for this, right?"

"Peukington will never believe Pistache," she remarked casually. "And, if they do believe that he can't remember anything, they will probably think he lost the coin. He's might very well be unconscious somewhere right now. Seriously."

"I suppose."

"When I saw him down that fish crap, that's when I decided to do it. What an idiot."

My mind raced. "I don't know. Let's say they do trace it back to us somehow. What do we do?"

"We won't have it."

"Honey," I laughed as I looked at the coin sitting in her hand. "How do you figure that? You want to sell it? They'll know."

"No, I don't think we should sell it."

"What then? Do you want to give it to a museum?"

"Not exactly," she said. "If we do that, Peukington winds up claiming it. He's rich and pretty famous. He'll just wind up getting it right back."

"So what's wrong with that?!"

"Pete, he literally tried to murder you. I don't want him to ever have it back."

"Well now I'm a little worried that he's going to try again."

"No listen," she said trying to calm me. "I've thought this through."

"Oh that's good to know," I said as my forehead immediately felt hot. "You've thought it through, have you? You've taken the last sleepless, drunk hour to really give it some solid rational thought?"

"Take it easy, Pete. Very funny."

"Okay," I brainstormed. "So we just leave it sitting somewhere maybe. We just walk away."

"Why would we do that?" Janie asked.

"I don't know. I'm thinking we'll just totally separate ourselves from it. We'll forget all about it."

Janie nodded as she considered it, finally maybe coming around.

"Besides," I continued, "someone new could maybe find it. That might be a nice next step in the life of the coin. After all, these kinds of histories never stop. It's only chapters that end."

"I guess," Janie said. "Only problem with that is they might also try to appraise it or sell it. That route probably finds its way back to Peukington, too."

"So what then? I don't get it. What's your plan?"

"Okay, hear me out," she began. "I am going to let it be your choice. The coin is my gift to you. But, I think you should consider throwing it off this bridge."

"Are you serious?! What good does that do?!" I exclaimed.

Janie grabbed my hand and thrust the coin into my palm. The energy in her eyes was obvious.

"You can do two things," she said. "If you want to keep it, I'm with you until the end. Maybe nothing happens. Maybe it just sits in a box on our bookshelf, and we can tell this story to other couples when they come over. The big punch line will be that we have the coin sitting right in our house. No one will believe us, but we'll know it happened, and it will be perfect."

I liked that idea but quickly found myself running through alternative scenarios.

"And maybe Peukington shows up, finds it, and his guys murder us," I offered.

"Maybe. Who knows? But that's pretty unlikely if Pistache can't remember anything. As far as Peukington and Renard are concerned, they watched him leave with it. Pistache will have a hard time selling his story to them."

I sighed. "Okay, what's my other option?"

"Stick with me on this. You can hold this piece of Paris in your hand right here for the last time. This thing has seen kings, revolution, an emperor, wars, and all that stuff. With this little time-traveler, you know that you were part of pure magic, woven into its story forever. Then, after you've taken a minute to think about all of that, you can aim for the sunrise, send it out over the water, and return it to the city that really owned it the whole time anyway."

I looked down at the coin as she spoke.

"We can still tell the story, Pete. It'll end even better this way."

"But it's worth so much," I stammered, conflicted.

"What more do we really need?"

She was right. As we stood on the Pont des Arts, I pictured letting it fly into the exploding Parisian morning and seeing it shimmer one last time before losing it in the bright orange. We might not even hear it hit the water.

Janie smiled at me, waiting. I loved the tone of her skin in the sunrise light. Her beautiful look conveyed that signature mischief that had brought us to this moment, and I was reminded again exactly why I'd fallen for her in the first place. Sensing my thoughts, she touched my forearm, still smiling.

I turned to the water, now overwhelmingly bright with the morning sun. Breathing deeply, my fist closed around the coin. I wound up, even then still not knowing if I'd truly ever be able to let it go.

Acknowledgements

This story took nearly two years to complete. I have enjoyed writing it and feel truly lucky that you, the reader, picked it up. Thank you for reading this book.

Mollie, your imprint is all over this from our exploration of Paris' nightlife to the coffee mug you gave me with the horses on it from which I sip as I write this. You inspire me, and I love you.

Cece and Josie, you're both perfect.

Jennifer Maxson (Mom), thank you for editing an early draft of this work. Your ideas were extremely valuable and helped me shape this into what it is now.

Lauren Lastowka, thank you so much for taking the time to go over the final draft the way you did. You polished this in a way I couldn't have. Can't wait to do some hanging out hopefully soon!

Thank you Jennifer Law and Griffen Tull for the original cover design. You exceeded my hopes. Jennifer, you're a true pro.

Speaking of the original cover, thank you to Jeff Smith and the bartenders at Brockway Pub in Carmel, Indiana. Your bar is awesome. Jeff, I think you have a career in hand modeling.

I'd like to thank the following family and friends, who all lent fresh eyes to this text when mine were extremely tired: Brad Koselke, Jay and Brynn Pendrak, Richard Hewett, and Dan Maloney. Thank you all for listening to me talk about this story, then actually taking time to read it. Your insights were super valuable.

Lastly, I must mention the memory of my aunt, Caryl Lloyd, who passed away during the process of writing this book. An educator, scholar, and author, she introduced me to Paris when I was 16. My love for the city is evident now, and I owe her much of my affection for France in general. I hope she would have enjoyed this work.

About the Author

Pres Maxson is an award-winning author.

Actually, let's think about this for a second. Award winning? Yeah, I guess. Let's look at the lifetime tally: Pres was a 1990 Presidential Physical Fitness Award recipient; was the all-time record holder for a time in the Mighty Munchkin Practice Sweepstakes for minutes spent practicing piano in high school; was crowned "Mr. DHS" in 1997; won the essay contest naming his father "University of Iowa Dad of the Year 2002"; was named to the Hawkeye Marching Band's Rank of Honor in back-to-back years; was named Employee of the Month in 2008 at work; and, most recently, in 2014 was recognized by his niece and nephews with an actual plaque for "ongoing dedication and unwavering pursuit of excellence in the field of awesomeness." Those are the greatest hits. So technically, yes. Pres Maxson is award-winning.

But, even the term "author" is loosely used for Pres. Sure, he's written stuff. Most notably, he has a degree in English from the great University of Iowa, and he's written professional copy for the last decade. But also: a smattering of unpublished little stories, blog posts, unanswered tweets at various public figures, hundreds of song lyrics, and countless grocery lists. He is into haiku also, having written thousands of low-quality poems (and four really okay ones) in the last two decades.

So sure, Pres Maxson is an award-winning author. Let's go ahead with that.

Made in the USA
San Bernardino, CA
04 July 2018